I0661661

Owen Wister

The Dragon of Wantley, His Rise, His Voracity and His Downfall

A Romance

Owen Wister

The Dragon of Wantley, His Rise, His Voracity and His Downfall
A Romance

ISBN/EAN: 9783337019600

Printed in Europe, USA, Canada, Australia, Japan

Cover: Foto ©Andreas Hilbeck / pixelio.de

More available books at **www.hansebooks**.com

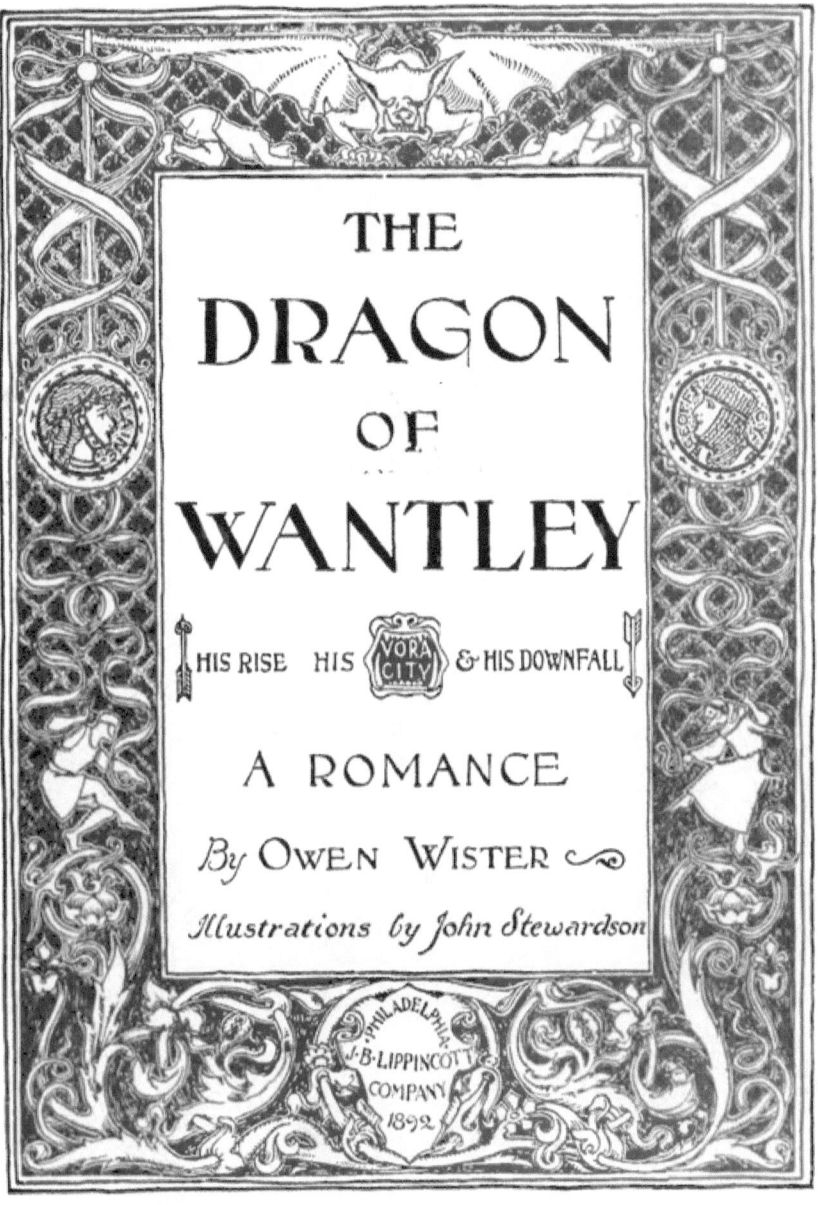

THE
DRAGON
OF
WANTLEY

HIS RISE HIS VORA CITY & HIS DOWNFALL

A ROMANCE

By OWEN WISTER

Illustrations by John Stewardson

PHILADELPHIA
J·B·LIPPINCOTT
COMPANY
1892

·COPYRIGHT· 1892·
·BY·J·B·LIPPINCOTT·COMPANY·
·PRINTED·BY·J·B·LIPPINCOTT·COMPANY·
·PHILADELPHIA·U·S·A·

TO

MY ANCIENT PLAYMATES IN APPIAN
WAY CAMBRIDGE THIS LIKELY
STORY IS DEDICATED FOR REASONS
BEST KNOWN TO THEMSELVES

Preface

When Betsinda held the Rose
    And the Ring decked Giglio's finger,
    Thackeray! 'twas sport to linger
With thy wise, gay-hearted prose.
Books were merry, goodness knows!
When Betsinda held the Rose.

Who but foggy drudglings doze
    While Rob Gilpin toasts thy witches,
    While the Ghost waylays thy breeches,
Ingoldsby? Such tales as those
Exorcised our peevish woes
When Betsinda held the Rose.

Realism, thou specious pose!
    Haply it is good we met thee;
    But, passed by, we'll scarce regret thee;
For we love the light that glows
Where Queen Fancy's pageant goes,
And Betsinda holds the Rose.

Shall we dare it? Then let's close
    Doors to-night on things statistic,
    Seek the hearth in circle mystic,
Till the conjured fire-light shows
Where Youth's bubbling Fountain flows,
And Betsinda holds the Rose.

7

TABLE OF CONTENTS

LIST OF ILLUSTRATIONS

NE QUI SAULTE SAULTE SERA

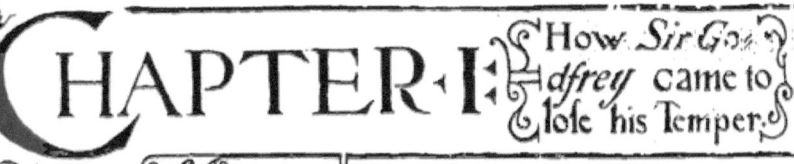

CHAPTER·I: How Sir Godfrey came to lose his Temper.

THE BVT LER HIS· BOY. GODFREY DISSEISIN.

HERE was something wrong in the cellar at Wantley Manor. Little Whelpdale knew it, for he was Buttons, and Buttons always knows what is being done with the wine, though he may look as if he did not. And old Popham knew it, too. He was Butler, and responsible to Sir Godfrey for all the brandy, and ale, and cider, and mead, and canary, and other strong waters there were in the house.

Now, Sir Godfrey Disseisin, fourth Baron of Wantley, and immediate tenant by knight-service to His Majesty King John of England, was particular about his dogs, and particular about his horses, and about his only daughter and his boy Roland, and had been very particular indeed about his wife, who, I am sorry to say, did not live long. But all this was nothing to the fuss he made about his wine. When the claret was not warm enough, or the Moselle wine was not cool enough, you could hear him roaring all over the house; for, though generous in heart and a staunch Churchman, he was immoderately choleric. Very often, when Sir Godfrey fell into one of his rages at dinner, old Popham, standing behind his chair, trembled so violently that his calves would shake loose, thus obliging him to hasten behind the tall leathern screen at the head of the banquet-hall and readjust them.

Twice in each year the Baron sailed over to France, where he visited the wine-merchants, and tasted samples of all new vintages, —though they frequently gave him unmentionable aches. Then,

2

when he was satisfied that he had selected the soundest and rich-
est, he returned to Wantley Manor, bringing home wooden casks
that were as big as hay-stacks, and so full they could not gurgle
when you tipped them. Upon arriving, he sent for Mrs. Mistletoe,
the family governess and (for economy's sake) housekeeper, who
knew how to write—something the Baron's father and mother had
never taught him when he was a little boy, because they didn't
know how themselves, and despised people who did,—and when
Mrs. Mistletoe had cut neat pieces of card-board for labels and got
ready her goose-quill, Sir Godfrey would say, "Write, Château
Lafitte, 1187;" or, "Write, Chambertin, 1203." (Those, you know,
were the names and dates of the vintages.) "Yes, my lord,"
Mistletoe always piped up; on which Sir Godfrey would peer over
her shoulder at the writing, and mutter, "Hum; yes, that's correct,"
just as if he knew how to read, the old humbug! Then Mistletoe,
who was a silly girl and had lost her husband early, would go
"Tee-hee, Sir Godfrey!" as the gallant gentleman gave her a kiss.
Of course, this was not just what he should have done ; but he was
a widower, you must remember, and besides that, as the years
went on this little ceremony ceased to be kept up. When it was
"Château Lafitte, 1187," kissing Mistletoe was one thing; but when
it came to "Chambertin, 1203," the lady weighed two hundred and
twenty-five pounds, and wore a wig.

But, wig and all, Mistletoe had a high position in Wantley
Manor. The household was conducted on strictly feudal principles.
Nobody, except the members of the family, received higher con-
sideration than did the old Governess. She and the Chaplain were
on a level, socially, and they sat at the same table with the Baron.
That drew the line. Old Popham the Butler might tell little
Whelpdale as often as he pleased that he was just as good as
Mistletoe; but he had to pour out Mistletoe's wine for her, notwith-
standing. If she scolded him, (which she always did if Sir Godfrey

had been scolding her,) do you suppose he dared to answer back? Gracious, no! He merely kicked the two head-footmen, Meeson and Welsby, and spoke severely to the nine housemaids. Meeson and Welsby then made life a painful thing for the five under footmen and the grooms, while the nine housemaids boxed the ears of Whelpdale the Buttons, and Whelpdale the Buttons punched the scullion's eye. As for the scullion, he was bottom of the list; but he could always relieve his feelings by secretly pulling the tails of Sir Godfrey's two tame ravens, whose names were Croak James and Croak Elizabeth. I never knew what these birds did at that; but something, you may be sure. So you see that I was right when I said the household was conducted on strictly feudal principles. The Cook had a special jurisdiction of her own, and everybody was more or less afraid of her.

Whenever Sir Godfrey had come home with new wine, and after the labels had been pasted on the casks, then Popham, with Whelpdale beside him, had these carefully set down in the cellar, which was a vast dim room, the ceilings supported by heavy arches; the barrels, bins, kegs, hogsheads, tuns, and demijohns of every size and shape standing like forests and piled to the ceiling. And now something was wrong there.

"This 'ere's a hawful succumstence, sir," observed Whelpdale the Buttons to his superior, respectfully.

"It is, indeed, a himbroglio," replied Popham, who had a wide command of words, and knew it.

Neither domestic spoke again for some time. They were seated in the buttery. The Butler crossed his right leg over his left, and waved the suspended foot up and down,—something he seldom did unless very grievously perturbed. As for poor little Whelpdale, he mopped his brow with the napkins that were in a basket waiting for the wash.

Then the bell rang.

"His ludship's study-bell," said Popham. "Don't keep him waiting."

"Hadn't you better apprise his ludship of the facks?" asked Whelpdale, in a weak voice.

Popham made no reply. He arose and briefly kicked Buttons out of the buttery. Then he mounted a chair to listen better. "He has hentered his ludship's apawtment," he remarked, hearing the sound of voices come faintly down the little private staircase that led from Sir Godfrey's study to the buttery: the Baron was in the habit of coming down at night for crackers and cheese before he went to bed. Presently one voice grew much louder than the other. It questioned. There came a sort of whining in answer. Then came a terrific stamp on the ceiling and a loud "Go on, sir!"

"Now, now, now!" thought Popham.

Do you want to hear at once, without waiting any longer, what little Whelpdale is telling Sir Godfrey? Well, you must know that for the past thirteen years, ever since 1190, the neighbourhood had been scourged by a terrible Dragon. The monster was covered with scales, and had a long tail and huge unnatural wings, beside fearful jaws that poured out smoke and flame whenever they opened. He always came at dead of night, roaring, bellowing, and sparkling and flaming over the hills, and horrid claps of thunder were very likely to attend his progress. Concerning the nature and quality of his roaring, the honest copyholders of Wantley could never agree, although every human being had heard him hundreds of times. Some said it was like a mad bull, only much louder and worse. Old Gaffer Piers the ploughman swore that if his tomcat weighed a thousand pounds it would make a noise almost as bad as that on summer nights, with the moon at the full and other cats handy. But farmer Stiles said, "Nay, 'tis like none of your bulls nor cats. But when I have come home too near the next morning, my wife can make me think of this Dragon as soon as ever her mouth be open."

This shows you that there were divers opinions. If you were not afraid to look out of the window about midnight, you could see the sky begin to look red in the quarter from which he was approaching, just as it glares when some distant house is on fire. But you must shut the window and hide before he came over the hill; for very few that had looked upon the Dragon ever lived to that day twelvemonth. This monster devoured the substance of the tenantry and yeomen. When their fields of grain were golden for the harvest, in a single night he cut them down and left their acres blasted by his deadly fire. He ate the cows, the sheep, the poultry, and at times even sucked eggs. Many pious saints had visited the district, but not one had been able by his virtue to expel the Dragon; and the farmers and country folk used to repeat a legend that said the Dragon was a punishment for the great wickedness of the Baron's ancestor,

Popham awaiteth the Result with Dignity

the original Sir Godfrey Disseisin, who, when summoned on the
first Crusade to Palestine, had entirely refused to go and help his
cousin Godfrey de Bouillon wrest the Holy Sepulchre from the
Paynim. The Baron's ancestor, when a stout young lad, had come
over with William the Conqueror; and you must know that to
have an ancestor who had come over with William the Conqueror
was in those old days a much rarer thing than it is now, and any
one who could boast of it was held in high esteem by his neighbours, who asked him to dinner and left their cards upon him
continually. But the first Sir Godfrey thought one conquest was
enough for any man; and in reply to his cousin's invitation to try
a second, answered in his blunt Norman French, "Nul tiel verte
dedans ccot oyle," which displeased the Church, and ended forever
all relations between the families. The Dragon did not come at
once, for this gentleman's son, the grandfather of our Sir Godfrey,
as soon as he was twenty-one, went off to the Holy Land himself,
fought very valiantly, and was killed, leaving behind him at Wantley an inconsolable little wife and an heir six months old. This
somewhat appeased the Pope; but the present Sir Godfrey, when
asked to accompany King Richard Lion Heart on his campaign
against the Infidel, did not avail himself of the opportunity to
set the family right in the matter of Crusades. This hereditary
impiety, which the Pope did not consider at all mended by the
Baron's most regular attendance at the parish church on all Sun-
days, feast days, fast days, high days, low days, saints' days, vigils,
and octaves, nor by his paying his tithes punctually to Father
Anselm, Abbot of Oyster-le-Main (a wonderful person, of whom I
shall have a great deal to tell you presently), this impiety, I say,
finished the good standing of the House of Wantley. Rome
frowned, the earth trembled, and the Dragon came. And (the
legend went on to say) this curse would not be removed until
a female lineal descendant of the first Sir Godfrey, a young lady

who had never been married, and had never loved anybody except
her father and mother and her sisters and brothers, should go out
in the middle of the night on Christmas Eve, all by herself, and
encounter the Dragon single handed.

Now, of course, this is not what little Whelpdale is trying to
tell the Baron up in the study; for everybody in Wantley knew all
about the legend except one person, and that was Miss Elaine, Sir
Godfrey's only daughter, eighteen years old at the last Court of
Piepoudre, when her father (after paying all the farmers for all the
cows and sheep they told him had been eaten by the Dragon since
the last Court) had made his customary proclamation, to wit: his
good-will and protection to all his tenantry; and if any man, woman,
child, or other person, caused his daughter, Miss Elaine, to hear
anything about the legend, such tale-bearer should be chained to a
tree, and kept fat until the Dragon found him and ate him. So
everybody obligingly kept the Baron's secret.

Sir Godfrey is just this day returned from France with some
famous tuns of wine, and presents for Elaine and Mrs. Mistletoe.
His humour is (or was, till Whelpdale, poor wretch! answered the
bell) of the best possible. And now, this moment, he is being told
by the luckless Buttons that the Dragon of Wantley has taken to
drinking, as well as eating, what does not belong to him; has for
the last three nights burst the big gates of the wine-cellar that
open on the hillside the Manor stands upon; that a hogshead of
the Baron's best Burgundy is going; and that two hogsheads of
his choicest Malvoisie are gone!

One hundred and twenty-eight gallons in three nights' work!
But I suppose a fire-breathing Dragon must be very thirsty.

There was a dead silence in the study overhead, and old Popham's calves were shaking loose as he waited.

"And so you stood by and let this black, sneaking, prowling,
thieving," (here the Baron used some shocking expressions which I

The Baron purfueth Whelpdale into the Buttery

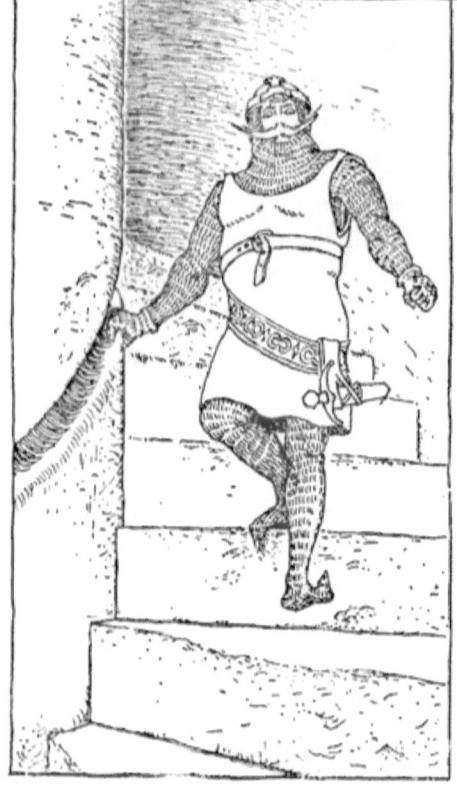

shall not set down) "Dragon swill my wine?"

"St—st—stood by, your ludship?" said little Whelpdale. "No, sir; no one didn't do any standing by, sir. He roared that terrible, sir, we was all under the bed."

"Now, by my coat of mail and great right leg!" shouted Sir Godfrey. The quaking Popham heard no more. The door of the private staircase flew open with a loud noise, and down came little Whelpdale head over heels into the buttery. After him strode Sir Godfrey in full mail armour, clashing his steel fists against the banisters. The nose-piece of his helmet was pushed up to allow him to speak plainly,—and most plainly did he speak, I can assure you, all the way down stairs, keeping his right eye glaring upon Popham in one corner of the buttery, and at the same time petrifying Whelpdale with his left. From father to son, the Disseisins had always been famous for the manner in which they could straddle their eyes; and in Sir Godfrey the family trait was very strongly marked.

Arrived at the bottom, he stopped for a moment to throw a

ham through the stained-glass window, and then made straight for Popham. But the head Butler was an old family servant, and had learned to know his place. With surprising agility he hopped on a table, so that Sir Godfrey's foot flew past its destined goal and caught a shelf that was loaded with a good deal of his wedding china. The Baron was far too dignified a person to take any notice of this mishap, and he simply strode on, out of the buttery, and so through the halls of the Manor, where all who caught even the most distant sight of his coming, promptly withdrew into the privacy of their apartments.

CHAPTER·II·

❧How his Daughter, *Miss Elaine,*
behaued in Confequence ☙

HE Baron walked on, his rage
mounting as he went, till presently
he began talking aloud to himself.
"Mort d'aieul and Cosenage!" he
muttered, grinding his teeth over
these oaths: "matters have come
to a pretty pass, per my and per
tout! And this is what my wine-
bibbing ancestor has brought on his posterity by his omission to
fight for the True Faith!"

Sir Godfrey knew the outrageous injustice of this remark as
well as you or I do; and so did the portrait of his ancestor, which
he happened to be passing under, for the red nose in the tapes-
try turned a deeper ruby in scornful anger. But, luckily for the
nerves of its descendant, the moths had eaten its mouth away so
entirely, that the retort it attempted to make sounded only like a
faint hiss, which the Baron mistook for a little gust of wind behind
the arras.

"My ruddy Burgundy!" he groaned, "going, going! and my
rich, fruity Malvoisie,—all gone! Father Anselm didn't appreciate
it, either, that night he dined here last September. He said I had
put egg-shells in it. Egg-shells! Pooh! As if any parson could
talk about wine. These Church folk had better mind their business, and say grace, and eat their dinner, and be thankful. That's
what I say. Egg-shells, forsooth!" The Baron was passing through

the chapel, and he mechanically removed his helmet; but he did
not catch sight of the glittering eye of Father Anselm himself,
who had stepped quickly into the confessional, and there in the
dark watched Sir Godfrey with a strange, mocking smile. When
he had the chapel to himself again, the tall gray figure of the
Abbot appeared in full view, and craftily moved across the place.
If you had been close beside him, and had listened hard, you
could have heard a faint clank and jingle beneath his gown as he
moved, which would have struck you as not the sort of noise a
hair-shirt ought to make. But I am glad you were not there;
for I do not like the way the Abbot looked at all, especially so
near Christmas-tide, when almost every one somehow looks kinder
as he goes about in the world. Father Anselm moved out of the
chapel, and passed through lonely corridors out of Wantley Manor,
out of the court-yard, and so took his way to Oyster-le-Main in
the gathering dusk. The few people who met him received his
blessing, and asked no questions; for they were all serfs of the
glebe, and well used to meeting the Abbot going and coming near
Wantley Manor.

Meanwhile, Sir Godfrey paced along. "To think," he continued,
aloud, "to think the country could be rid of this monster, this guz-
zling serpent, in a few days! Plenty would reign again. Public
peace of mind would be restored. The cattle would increase, the
crops would grow, my rents treble, and my wines be drunk no
more by a miserable, ignorant—but, no! I'm her father. Elaine
shall never be permitted to sacrifice herself for one dragon, or
twenty dragons, either."

"Why, what's the matter, papa?"

Sir Godfrey started. There was Miss Elaine in front of him;
and she had put on one of the new French gowns he had brought
over with him.

"Matter? Plenty of matter!" he began, unluckily. "At least,

nothing is the matter at all, my dear. What a question! Am I
not back all safe from the sea? Nothing is the matter, of course!
Hasn't your old father been away from you two whole months?
And weren't those pretty dresses he has carried back with him
for his little girl? And isn't the wine—Zounds, no, the wine isn't
—at least, certainly it is—to be sure it's what it ought to be
—*what* it ought to be? Yes! But, Mort d'aieul! not *where* it
ought to be! Hum! hum! I think I am going mad!" And Sir
Godfrey, forgetting he held the helmet all this while, dashed his
hands to his head with such violence that the steel edge struck
hard above the ear, and in one minute had raised a lump there
as large as the egg of a fowl.

"Poor, poor papa," said Miss Elaine. And she ran and fetched
some cold water, and, dipping her dainty lace handkerchief into it,
she bathed the Baron's head.

"Thank you, my child," he murmured, presently. "Of course,
nothing is the matter. They were very slow in putting the new"
(here he gave a gulp) "casks of wine into the cellar; that's all.
'Twill soon be dinner-time. I must make me ready."

And so say-
ing, the Baron
kissed his
daughter and
strode away
towards his
dressing-room.
But she heard
him shout
"Mort d'aieul!"

Sir Godfrey maketh him
ready for the Bath

more than once before he was out of hearing. Then his dressing-room door shut with a bang, and sent echoes all along the entries above and below.

The December night was coming down, and a little twinkling lamp hung at the end of the passage. Towards this Miss Elaine musingly turned her steps, still squeezing her now nearly dry handkerchief.

"What did he mean?" she said to herself.

"Elaine!" shouted Sir Godfrey, away off round a corner.

"Yes, papa, I'm coming."

"Don't come. I'm going to the bath. A—did you hear me say anything particular?"

"Do you mean when I met you?" answered Elaine. "Yes—no—that is,—not exactly, papa."

"Then don't dare to ask me any questions, for I won't have it." And another door slammed.

"What did papa mean?" said Miss Elaine, once more.

Her bright brown eyes were looking at the floor as she walked slowly on towards the light, and her lips, which had been a little open so that you could have seen what dainty teeth she had, shut quite close. In fact, she was thinking, which was something you could seldom accuse her of. I do not know exactly what her thoughts were, except that the words "dragon" and "sacrifice" kept bumping against each other in them continually; and when-ever they bumped, Miss Elaine frowned a little deeper, till she really looked almost solemn. In this way she came under the hanging lamp and entered the door in front of which it shone.

This was the ladies' library, full of the most touching romances about Roland, and Walter of Aquitaine, and Sir Tristram, and a great number of other excitable young fellows, whose behaviour had invariably got them into dreadful difficulties, but had as invari-ably made them, in the eyes of every damsel they saw, the most

SIR·GODFREY·Setteth·in·to·hys·Bath·

attractive, fascinating, sweet, dear creatures in the world. Nobody
ever read any of these books except Mrs. Mistletoe and the family
Chaplain. These two were, indeed, the only people in the household that knew how to read,—which may account for it in some
measure. It was here that Miss Elaine came in while she was
thinking so hard, and found old Mistletoe huddled to the fire.
She had been secretly reading the first chapters of a new and
pungent French romance, called "Roger and Angelica," that was
being published in a Paris and a London magazine simultaneously.
Only thus could the talented French author secure payment for his
books in England; for King John, who had recently murdered his
little nephew Arthur, had now turned his attention to obstructing

all arrangements for an international copyright. In many respects,
this monarch was no credit to his family.

When the Governess heard Miss Elaine open the door behind
her, she thought it was the family Chaplain, and, quickly throwing
the shocking story on the floor, she opened the household cookery-
book,—an enormous volume many feet square, suspended from the
ceiling by strong chains, and containing several thousand receipts
for English, French, Italian, Croatian, Dalmatian, and Acarnanian
dishes, beginning with a poem in blank verse written to his confec-
tioner by the Emperor Charles the Fat. German cooking was
omitted.

"I'm looking up a new plum-pudding for Christmas," said
Mistletoe, nervously, keeping her virtuous eyes on the volume.

"Ah, indeed!" Miss Elaine answered, indifferently. She was
thinking harder than ever—was, in fact, inventing a little plan.

"Oh, so it's you, deary!" cried the Governess, much relieved.
She had feared the Chaplain might pick up the guilty magazine and
find its pages cut only at the place where the French story was.
And I am grieved to have to tell you that this is just what he did
do later in the evening, and sat down in his private room and read
about Roger and Angelica himself.

"Here's a good one," said Mistletoe. "Number 39, in the
Appendix to Part Fourth. Chop two pounds of leeks and——"

"But I may not be here to taste it," said Elaine.

"Bless the child!" said Mistletoe. "And where else would you
be on Christmas-day but in your own house?"

"Perhaps far away. Who knows?"

"You haven't gone and seen a young man and told him——"

"A young man, indeed!" said Elaine, with a toss of her head.
"There's not a young man in England I would tell anything save
to go about his business."

Miss Elaine had never seen any young men except when they

ISTLETOE · CONSVLTETH · Y^e
COOKYNGE · BOOKE·

came to dine on Sir Godfrey's invitation ; and his manner on those occasions so awed them that they always sat on the edge of their chairs, and said, "No, thank you," when the Baron said, "Have some more capon?" Then the Baron would snort, "Nonsense! Popham, bring me Master Percival's plate," upon which Master Percival invariably simpered, and said that really he did believe he *would* take another slice. After these dinners, Miss Elaine retired to her own part of the house ; and that was all she ever saw of young men, whom she very naturally deemed a class to be despised as silly and wholly lacking in self-assertion.

"Then where in the name of good saints are you going to be?" Mistletoe went on.

"Why," said Elaine, slowly (and here she looked very slyly at the old Governess, and then quickly appeared to be considering the lace on her dress), "why, of course, papa would not permit me to sacrifice myself for one dragon or twenty dragons."

"What!" screamed Mistletoe, all in a flurry (for she was a fool). "What?"

"Of course, I know papa would say that," said Miss Elaine, demure as possible.

"Oh, mercy me!" squeaked Mistletoe ; "we are undone!"

"To be sure, I might agree with papa," said the artful thing, knowing well enough she was on the right track.

"Oo—oo!" went the Governess, burying her nose in the household cookery-book and rocking from side to side.

"But then I might not agree with papa, you know. I might think,—might think——" Miss Elaine stopped at what she might think, for really she hadn't the slightest idea what to say next.

"You have no right to think,—no right at all!" burst out Mistletoe. "And you sha'n't be allowed to think. I'll tell Sir Godfrey at once, and he'll forbid you. Oh, dear! oh, dear! just before Christmas Eve, too! The only night in the year! She has no time to change her mind; and she'll be eaten up if she goes, I know she will. What villain told you of this, child? Let me know, and he shall be punished at once."

"I shall not tell you that," said Elaine.

"Then everybody will be suspected," moaned Mistletoe. "Everybody. The whole household. And we shall all be thrown to the Dragon. Oh, dear! was there ever such a state of things?" The Governess betook herself to weeping and wringing her hands, and Elaine stood watching her and wondering how in the world she could find out more. She knew now just enough to keep her from eating or sleeping until she knew everything.

"I don't agree with papa, at all," she said, during a lull in the tears. This was the only remark she could think of.

"He'll lock you up, and feed you on bread and water till you do—oo—oo!" sobbed Mistletoe; "and by that time we shall all be ea—ea—eaten up!"

"But I'll talk to papa, and make him change his mind."

"He won't. Do you think you're going to make him care more about a lot of sheep and cows than he does about his only daughter? Doesn't he pay the people for everything the Dragon eats up? Who would pay him for you, when you were eaten up?"

"How do you know that I should be eaten up?" asked Miss Elaine.

"Oh, dear! oh, dear! and how could you stop it? What could a girl do alone against a dragon in the middle of the night?"

"But on Christmas Eve?" suggested the young lady. "There might be something different about that. He might feel better, you know, on Christmas Eve."

"Do you suppose a wicked, ravenous dragon with a heathen tail is going to care whether it is Christmas Eve or not? He'd have you for his Christmas dinner, and that's all the notice he would take of the day. And then perhaps he wouldn't leave the country, after all. How can you be sure he would go away, just because that odious, vulgar legend says so? Who would rely on a dragon? And so there you would be gone, and he would be here, and everything!"

Mistletoe's tears flowed afresh; but you see she had said all that Miss Elaine was so curious to know about, and the fatal secret was out.

The Quarter-Bell rang for dinner, and both the women hastened to their rooms to make ready; Mistletoe still boo-hooing and snuffling, and declaring that she had always said some wretched, abominable villain would tell her child about that horrid, ridiculous legend, that was a perfect falsehood, as anybody could see, and very likely invented by the Dragon himself, because no human being with any feelings at all would think of such a cruel, absurd idea; and if they ever did, they deserved to be eaten themselves; and she would not have it.

She said a great deal more that Elaine, in the next room, could not hear (though the door was open between), because the Governess put her fat old face under the cold water in the basin, and, though she went on talking just the same, it only produced an angry sort of bubbling, which conveyed very little notion of what she meant.

ELAINE · MAKETH · AN · VNEXPECTED · REMARK

So they descended the stairway, Miss Elaine walking first, very straight and solemn; and that was the way she marched into the banquet-hall, where Sir Godfrey waited.

"Papa," said she; "I think I'll meet the Dragon on Christmas Eve!"

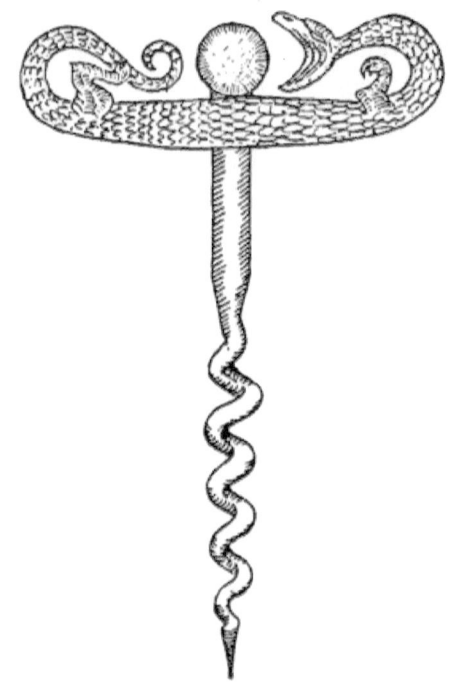

CHAPTER·III

C Reueals the *Dragon* in his Den

ROUND the sullen towers of Oyster-le-Main the snow was falling steadily. It was slowly banking up in the deep sills of the windows, and Hubert the Sacristan had given up sweeping the steps. Patches of it, that had collected on the top of the great bell as the slanting draughts blew it in through the belfry-window, slid down from time to time among the birds which had nestled for shelter in the beams below. From the heavy main outer-gates, the country spread in a white unbroken sheet to the woods. Twice, perhaps, through the morning had wayfarers toiled by along the nearly-obliterated high-road.

"Good luck to the holy men!" each had said to himself as he looked at the chill and austere walls of the Monastery. "Good luck! and I hope that within there they be warmer than I am." Then I think it very likely that as he walked on, blowing the fingers of the hand that held his staff, he thought of his fireside and his wife, and blessed Providence for not making him pious enough to be a monk and a bachelor.

This is what was doing in the world outside. Now inside the stone walls of Oyster-le-Main, whose grim solidity spoke of narrow cells and of pious knees continually bent in prayer, not a monk paced the corridors, and not a step could be heard above or below in the staircase that wound up through the round towers.

Silence was everywhere, save that from a remote quarter of the
Monastery came a faint sound of music. Upon such a time as
Christmas Eve, it might well be that carols in plenty would be
sung or studied by the saintly men. But this sounded like no
carol. At times the humming murmur of the storm drowned the
measure, whatever it was, and again it came along the dark, cold
entries, clearer than before. Away in a long vaulted room, whose
only approach was a passage in the thickness of the walls, safe
from the intrusion of the curious, a company is sitting round a
cavernous chimney, where roars and crackles a great blazing heap
of logs. Surely, for a monkish song, their melody is most odd;
yet monks they are, for all are clothed in gray, like Father Anselm,
and a rope round the waist of each. But what can possibly be
in that huge silver rundlet into which they plunge their goblets so
often? The song grows louder than ever.

> We are the monks of Oyster-le-Main,
> Hooded and gowned as fools may see;
> Hooded and gowned though we monks be,
> Is that a reason we should abstain
> From cups of the gamesome Burgundie?
>
> Though our garments make it plain
> That we are Monks of Oyster-le-Main,
> That is no reason we should abstain
> From cups of the gamesome Burgundie.

"I'm sweating hot," says one. "How for disrobing, brothers?
No danger on such a day as this, foul luck to the snow!"

Which you see was coarse and vulgar language for any one to
be heard to use, and particularly so for a godly celibate. But the
words were scarce said, when off fly those monks' hoods, and the
waist-ropes rattle as they fall on the floor, and the gray gowns
drop down and are kicked away.

Every man jack of them is in black armour, with a long sword buckled to his side.

"Long cheer to the Guild of Go-as-you-Please!" they shouted, hoarsely, and dashed their drinking-horns on the board. Then filled them again.

"Give us a song, Hubert," said one. "The day's a dull one out in the world."

"Wait a while," replied Hubert, whose nose was hidden in his cup; "this new Wantley tipple is a vastly comfortable brew. What d'ye call the stuff?"

"Malvoisie, thou oaf!" said another; "and of a delicacy many degrees above thy bumpkin palate. Leave profaning it, therefore, and to thy refrain without more ado."

"Most unctuous sir," replied Hubert, "in demanding me this

favour, you seem forgetful that the juice of Pleasure is sweeter than the milk of Human Kindness. I'll not sing to give thee an opportunity to outnumber me in thy cups."

And he filled and instantly emptied another sound bumper of the Malvoisie, lurching slightly as he did so. "Health!" he added, preparing to swallow the next.

"A murrain on such pagan thirst!" exclaimed he who had been toasted, snatching the cup away. "Art thou altogether unslakable? Is thy belly a lime-kiln? Nay, shalt taste not a single drop more, Hubert, till we have a stave. Come, tune up, man!"

"Give me but leave to hold the empty vessel, then," the singer pleaded, falling on one knee in mock supplication.

"Accorded, thou sot!" laughed the other. "Carol away, now!"

They fell into silence, each replenishing his drinking-horn. The snow beat soft against the window, and from outside, far above them, sounded the melancholy note of the bell ringing in the hour for meditation.

So Hubert began:

When the sable veil of night
　　Over hill and glen is spread,
The yeoman bolts his door in fright,
　　And he quakes within his bed.
Far away on his ear
　　There strikes a sound of dread:
Something comes! it is here!
　　It is passed with awful tread.
There's a flash of unholy flame;
　　There is smoke hangs hot in the air:
'Twas the Dragon of Wantley came:
　　Beware of him, beware!

　　But we beside the fire
　　　　Sit close to the steaming bowl;
　　We pile the logs up higher,
　　　　And loud our voices roll.

When the yeoman wakes at dawn
　　To begin his round of toil,
His garner's bare, his sheep are gone,
　　And the Dragon holds the spoil.

All day long through the earth
  That yeoman makes his moan:
All day long there is mirth
  Behind these walls of stone.
For we are the Lords of Ease,
  The gaolers of carking Care,
The Guild of Go-as-you-Please!
  Beware of us, beware!

So we beside the fire
  Sit down to the steaming bowl:
We pile the logs up higher,
  And loud our voices roll.

The roar of twenty lusty throats and the clatter of cups banging on the table rendered the words of the chorus entirely inaudible.

"Here's Malvoisie for thee, Hubert," said one of the company, dipping into the rundlet. But his hand struck against the dry bottom. They had finished four gallons since breakfast, and it was scarcely eleven gone on the clock!

"Oh, I am betrayed!" Hubert sang out. Then he added, "But there is a plenty where that came from." And with that he reached for his gown, and, fetching out a bunch of great brass keys, proceeded towards a tall door in the wall, and turned the lock. The door swung open, and Hubert plunged into the dark recess thus disclosed. An exclamation of chagrin followed, and the empty hide of a huge crocodile, with a pair of trailing wings to it, came bumping out from the closet into the hall, giving out many hollow cracks as it floundered along, fresh from a vigourous kick that the intemperate minstrel had administered in his rage at having put his hand into the open jaws of the monster instead of upon the neck of the demijohn that contained the Malvoisie.

"Beshrew thee, Hubert!" said the voice of a new-comer, who stood eyeing the proceedings from a distance, near where he had entered; "treat the carcase of our patron saint with a more befitting reverence, or I'll have thee caged and put upon bread and water. Remember, that whosoever kicks that skin in some sort kicks me."

"Long life to the Dragon of Wantley!" said Hubert, reappearing, very dusty, but clasping a plump demijohn.

"Hubert, my lad," said the new-comer, "put back that vessel of inebriation: and, because I like thee well for thy youth and thy sweet voice, do not therefore presume too far with me."

A somewhat uneasy pause followed upon this; and while Hubert edged back into the closet with his demijohn, Father Anselm frowned slightly as his eyes turned upon the scene of late hilarity.

But where is the Dragon in his den? you ask. Are we not coming to him soon? Ah, but we have come to him. You shall hear the truth. Never believe that sham story about More of More Hall, and how he slew the Dragon of Wantley. It is a gross fabrication of some unscrupulous and mediocre literary person, who, I make no doubt, was in the pay of More to blow his trumpet so loud that a credulous posterity might hear it. My account of the Dragon is the only true one.

So we are beside the Fire Sit close to the gleaming Bowl

CHAPTER·IV

I N those days of shifting fortunes, of turbulence and rapine, of knights-errant and minstrels seeking for adventure and love, and of solitary pilgrims and bodies of pious men wandering over Europe to proclaim that the duty of all was to arise and quell the pagan defilers of the Holy Shrine, good men and bad men, undoubted saints and unmistakable sinners, drifted forward and back through every country, came by night and by day to every household, and lived their lives in that unbounded and peril-ous freedom that put them at one moment upon the top limit of their ambition or their delight, and plunged them into violent and bloody death almost ere the moment was gone. It was a time when "fatten at thy neighbour's expense" was the one command-ment observed by many who outwardly maintained a profound respect for the original ten ; and any man whose wit taught him how this commandment could be obeyed with the greatest profit and the least danger was in high standing among his fellows.

Hence it was that Francis Almoign, Knight of the Voracious Stomach, cumbered with no domestic ties worthy of mention, a tall slim fellow who knew the appropriate hour to slit a throat or to wheedle a maid, came to be Grand Marshal of the Guild of Go-as-you-Please.

This secret band, under its Grand Marshal, roved over Europe and thrived mightily. Each member was as stout hearted a villain

51

as you could see. Sometimes their doings came to light, and they were forced to hasten across the borders of an outraged territory into new pastures. Yet they fared well in the main, for they could fight and drink and sing; and many a fair one smiled upon them, in spite of their perfectly outrageous morals.

So, one day, they came into the neighbourhood of Oyster-le-Main, where much confusion reigned among the good monks. Sir Godfrey Disseisin over at Wantley had let Richard Lion Heart depart for the Holy Wars without him. "Like father like son," the people muttered in their discontent. "Sure, the Church will gravely punish this second offence." To all these whisperings of rumour the Grand Marshal of the Guild paid fast attention; for he was a man who laid his plans deeply, and much in advance of the event. He saw the country was fat and the neighbours foolish. He took note of the handsome tithes that came in to Oyster-le-Main for the support of the monks. He saw all these things, and set himself to thinking.

Upon a stormy afternoon, when the light was nearly gone out of the sky, a band of venerable pilgrims stood at the great gates of the Monastery. Their garments were tattered, their shoes were in sad disrepair. They had walked (they said) all the way from Jerusalem. Might they find shelter for the night? The tale they told, and the mere sight of their trembling old beards, would have melted hearts far harder than those which beat in the breasts of the monks of Oyster-le-Main. But above all, these pilgrims brought with them as convincing proofs of their journey a collection of relics and talismans (such as are to be met with only in Eastern countries), of great wonder and virtue. With singular generosity, which they explained had been taught them by the Arabs, they presented many of these treasures to the delighted inmates of the Monastery, who hastened to their respective cells,— this one reverently cherishing a tuft of hair from the tail of one

of Daniel's lions; another handling with deep fervour a strip of
the coat of many colours once worn by the excellent Joseph. But
the most extraordinary relic among them all, was the skin of a
huge lizard beast, the like of which none in England had ever
seen. This, the Pilgrims told their hosts, was no less a thing
than a crocodile from the Nile, the renowned river of Moses. It
had been pressed upon them, as they were departing from the
City of Damascus, by a friend, a blameless chiropodist, whose
name was Omar Khayyam. He it was who eked out a pious
groat by tending the feet of all outward and inward bound pilgrims. Seated at the entrance of his humble booth, with the foot
of some holy man in his lap, he would speak words of kindness
and wisdom as he reduced the inflammation. One of his quaintest
sayings was, "If the Pope has bid thee wear hair next thy bare
skin, my son, why clap a wig over thy shaven scalp." So the
monks in proper pity and kindness, when they had shut the great
gates as night came down, made their pilgrim guests welcome to
bide at Oyster-le-Main as long as they pleased. The solemn bell
for retiring rolled forth in the darkness with a single deep clang,
and the sound went far and wide over the neighbouring district.
Those peasants who were still awake in their scattered cottages,
crossed themselves as they thought, "The holy men at Oyster-le-
Main are just now going to their rest."

And thus the world outside grew still, and the thick walls of
the Monastery loomed up against the stars.

Deep in the midnight, many a choking cry rang fearfully
through the stony halls, but came not to the outer air; and
the waning moon shone faintly down upon the enclosure of the
garden, where worked a band of silent grave-diggers, clad in
black armour, and with blood-red hands. The good country folk,
who came at early morning with their presents of poultry and
milk, little guessed what sheep's clothing the gray cowls and

gowns of Oyster-le-Main had become in a single night, nor what
impious lips those were which now muttered blessings over their
bent heads.

The following night, hideous sounds were heard in the fields,
and those who dared to open their shutters to see what the matter
was, beheld a huge lizard beast, with fiery breath and accompanied
by rattling thunder, raging over the soil, which he hardly seemed
to touch!

In this manner did the dreaded Dragon of Wantley make his
appearance, and in this manner did Sir Francis Almoign, Knight of
the Voracious Stomach, stand in the shoes of that Father Anselm
whom he had put so comfortably out of the way under the flower-
beds in the Monastery garden,—and never a soul in the world
except his companions in orgy to know the difference. He even
came to be welcome at Sir Godfrey's table; for after the Dragon's
appearance, the Baron grew civil to all members of the Church.
By day this versatile sinner, the Grand Marshal, would walk in
the sight of the world with staid step, clothed in gray, his hood
concealing his fierce, unchurchly eyes; by night, inside the crocodile
skin, he visited what places he chose, unhindered by the terrified
dwellers, and after him came his followers of the Guild to steal
the plunder and bear it back inside the walls of Oyster-le-Main.
Never in all their adventures had these superb miscreants been in
better plight: but now the trouble had begun, as you are going
to hear. We return to Hubert and the company.

"Hubert and all of you," said Father Anselm, or rather Sir
Francis, the Grand Marshal, as we know him to be. "they say
that whom the gods desire to destroy, him do they first make
drunk with wine."

"The application! the application!" they shouted in hoarse and
mirthful chorus, for they were certainly near that state favourable
to destruction by the gods. One black fellow with a sliding gait

Hubert Looketh out of y^e Window

ran into the closet and brought a sheet of thin iron, and a strange torch-like tube, which he lighted at the fire and blew into from the other end. A plume of spitting flame immediately shot far into the air.

"Before thy sermon proceeds, old Dragon," he said, puffing unsteady but solemn breaths between his words, "wrap up in lightning and thunder that we may be—may be—lieve what you say." Then he shook the iron till it gave forth a frightful shattering sound. The Grand Marshal said not a word. With three long steps he stood towering in front of the man and dealt him a side blow under the ear with his steel fist. He fell instantly, folding together like something boneless, and lay along the floor for a moment quite still, except that some piece in his armour made a light rattling as though there were muscles that quivered beneath

it. Then he raised himself slowly to a bench where his brothers
sat waiting, soberly enough. Only young Hubert grinned aside to
his neighbour, who, perceiving it, kept his eyes fixed as far from
that youth as possible.

"Thy turn next, if art not careful, Hubert," said Sir Francis
very quietly, as he seated himself.

"Wonder of saints!" Hubert thought secretly, not moving at
all, "how could he have seen that?"

"'Tis no small piece of good fortune," continued the Grand
Marshal, "that some one among us can put aside his slavish
appetites, and keep a clear eye on the watch against misadventure.
Here is my news. That hotch-pot of lies we set going among the
people has fallen foul of us. The daughter of Sir Godfrey has
heard our legend, and last week told her sire that to-night she
would follow it out to the letter, and meet the Dragon of Wantley
alone in single combat."

"Has she never loved any man?" asked one.

"She fulfils every condition."

"Who told her?"

"That most consummate of fools, the Mistletoe," said the
Grand Marshal.

"What did Sir Godfrey do upon that?" inquired Hubert.

"He locked up his girl and chained the Governess to a rock,
where she has remained in deadly terror ever since, but kept fat
for me to devour her. Me!" and Sir Francis permitted himself
to smile, though not very broadly.

"How if Sir Dragon had found the maid chained instead of the
ancient widow?" Hubert said, venturing to tread a little nearer to
familiarity on the strength of the amusement which played across
the Grand Master's face.

"Ah, Hubert boy," he replied, "I see it is not in the Spring
only, but in Autumn and Summer and Winter as well, that thy

fancy turns to thoughts of love. Did the calendar year but
contain a fifth season, in that also wouldst thou be making honey-
dew faces at somebody."

But young Hubert only grinned, and closed his flashing eyes a
little, in satisfaction at the character which had been given him.

"Time presses," Sir Francis said. "By noon we shall receive
an important visit. There has been a great sensation at Wantley.
The country folk are aroused; the farmers have discovered that
the secret of our legend has been revealed to Miss Elaine. Not
one of the clowns would have dared reveal it himself, but all
rejoice in the bottom of their hearts that she knows it, and
chooses to risk battle with the Dragon. Their honest Saxon
minds perceive the thrift of such an arrangement. Therefore there
is general anxiety and disturbance to know if Sir Godfrey will
permit the conflict. The loss of his Malvoisie tried him sorely,—
but he remains a father."

"That's kind in him," said Hubert.

Sir Francis turned a cold eye on Hubert. "As befits a
clean-blooded man," he proceeded, "I have risen at the dawn
and left you wine-pots in your thick sleep. From the wood's edge
over by Wantley I've watched the Baron come eagerly to an
upper window in his white night-shift. And when he looks out
on Mistletoe and sees she is not devoured, he bursts into a rage
that can be plainly seen from a distance. These six mornings I
laughed so loud at this spectacle, that I almost feared discovery.
Next, the Baron visits his daughter, only to find her food untasted
and herself silent. I fear she is less of a fool than the rest. But
now his paternal heart smites him, and he has let her out. Also
the Governess is free."

"Such a girl as that would not flinch from meeting our Dragon,"
said Hubert; "aye, or from seeking him."

"She must never meet the Dragon," Sir Francis declared.

"What could I do shut up in the crocodile, and she with a sword, of course?"

They were gloomily silent.

"I could not devour her properly as a dragon should. Nor could I carry her away," pursued Sir Francis.

Here Hubert, who had gone to the window, returned hastily, exclaiming, "They are coming!"

"Who are coming?" asked several.

"The Baron, his daughter, the Governess, and all Wantley at their backs, to ask our pious advice," said the Grand Marshal. "Quick, into your gowns, one and all! Be monks outside, though you stay men underneath." For a while the hall was filled with jostling gray figures entangled in the thick folds of the gowns, into which the arms, legs, and heads had been thrust regardless of direction; the armour clashed invisible underneath as the hot and choked members of the Guild plunged about like wild animals sewed into sacks, in their struggles to reappear in decent monastic attire. The winged crocodile was kicked into the closet, after it were hurled the thunder machine and the lightning torch, and after them clattered the cups and the silver rundlet. Barely had Hubert turned the key, when knocking at the far-off gate was heard.

"Go down quickly, Hubert," said the Grand Marshal, "and lead them all here."

Presently the procession of laity, gravely escorted by Hubert, began to file into the now barren-looking room, while the monks stood with hands folded, and sang loudly what sounded to the uninstructed ears of each listener like a Latin hymn.

CHAPTER V

SIR·GODFREY

WITH the respect that was due to holy men, Sir Godfrey removed his helmet, and stood waiting in a decent attitude of attention to the hymn, although he did not understand a single word of it. The long deliberate Latin words rolled out very grand to his ear, and, to tell you the truth, it is just as well his scholarship was faulty, for this is the English of those same words:

"It is my intention
To die in a tavern,
With wine in the neighbourhood,
Close by my thirsty mouth;
That angels in chorus
May sing, when they reach me,—
'Let Bacchus be merciful
Unto this wine-bibber.'"

But so devoutly did the monks dwell upon the syllables, so earnestly were the arms of each one folded against his breast, that you would never have suspected any unclerical sentiments were being expressed. The proximity of so many petticoats and kirtles caused considerable restlessness to Hubert; but he felt the burning eye of the Grand Marshal fixed upon him, and sang away with all his might.

61

Sir Godfrey began to grow impatient.

"Hem!" he said, moving his foot slightly.

This proceeding, however, was without result. The pious chant continued to resound, and the monks paid not the least attention to their visitors, but stood up together in a double line, vociferating Latin with as much zest as ever.

"Mort d'aïeul!" growled Sir Godfrey, shifting his other foot, and not so gingerly this second time.

By chance the singing stopped upon the same instant, so that the Baron's remark and the noise his foot had made sounded all over the room. This disconcerted him; for he felt his standing with the Church to be weak, and he rolled his eyes from one side to the other, watching for any effect his disturbance might have made. But, with the breeding of a true man of the world, the Grand Marshal merely observed, "Benedicite, my son!"

"Good-morning, Father," returned Sir Godfrey.

"And what would you with me?" pursued the so-called Father Anselm. "Speak, my son."

"Well, the fact is——" the Baron began, marching forward; but he encountered the eye of the Abbot, where shone a cold surprise at this over-familiar fashion of speech; so he checked himself, and, in as restrained a voice as he could command, told his story. How his daughter had determined to meet the Dragon, and so save Wantley; how nothing that a parent could say had influenced her intentions in the least; and now he placed the entire matter in the hands of the Church.

"Which would have been more becoming if you had done it at the first," said Father Anselm, reprovingly. Then he turned to Miss Elaine, who all this while had been looking out of the window with the utmost indifference.

"How is this, my daughter?" he said gravely, in his deep voice.

"Oh, the dear blessed man!" whispered Mistletoe, admiringly, to herself.

"It is as you hear, Father," said Miss Elaine, keeping her eyes away.

"And why do you think that such a peril upon your part would do away with this Dragon?"

"Says not the legend so?" she replied.

"And what may the legend be, my daughter?"

With some surprise that so well informed a person as Father Anselm should be ignorant of this prominent topic of the day, Sir Godfrey here broke in and narrated the legend to him with many vigourous comments.

"Ah, yes," said the Father, smiling gently when the story was done : "I do now remember that some such child's tale was in the mouths of the common folk once : but methought the nonsense was dead long since."

"The nonsense, Father!" exclaimed Elaine.

"Of a surety, my child. Dost suppose that Holy Church were so unjust as to visit the sins of thy knightly relatives upon the head of any weak woman, who is not in the order of creation designed for personal conflict with men, let alone dragons?"

"Bravo, Dragon!" thought Hubert, as he listened to this wily talk of his chief.

But the words "weak woman" had touched the pride of Miss Elaine. "I know nothing of weak women," she said, very stately ; "but I do know that I am strong enough to meet this Dragon, and, moreover, firmly intend to do so this very night."

"Peace, my daughter," said the monk : "and listen to the voice of thy mother the Church speaking through the humblest of her servants. This legend of thine holds not a single grain of truth. 'Tis a conceit of the common herd, set afoot by some ingenious fellow who may have thought he was doing a great thing in

devising such fantastic mixture. True it is that the Monster is a
visitation to punish the impiety of certain members of thy family.
True it is that he will not depart till a member of that family
perform a certain act. But it is to be a male descendant."

Now Sir Godfrey's boy Roland was being instructed in knightly
arts and conduct away from home.

"Who told you that?" inquired the Baron, as the thought of
his precious wine-cellar came into his head.

"On last Christmas Eve I had a vision," replied Father Anselm.
"Thy grandfather, the brave youth who by journeying to the
Holy War averted this curse until thine own conduct caused it
to descend upon us, appeared to me in shining armour. 'Anselm,'
he said, and raised his right arm, 'the Dragon is a grievous burden
on the people. I can see that from where I am. Now, Anselm,
when the fitting hour shall come, and my great-grandson's years
be mature enough to have made a man of him, let him go to the
next Holy War that is proclaimed, and on the very night of his
departure the curse will be removed and our family forgiven.
More than this, Anselm, if any male descendant from me direct
shall at any time attend a Crusade when it is declared, the country
will be free forever.' So saying, he dissolved out of my sight in
a silver gleaming mist." Here Father Anselm paused, and from
under his hood watched with a trifle of anxiety the effect of his
speech.

There was a short silence, and then Sir Godfrey said, "Am I
to understand this thing hangs on the event of another Crusade?"

The Abbot bowed.

"Meanwhile, till that event happen, the Dragon can rage
unchecked?"

The Abbot bowed again.

"Will there be another Crusade along pretty soon?" Sir Godfrey pursued.

"These things lie not in human knowledge," replied Father Anselm. He little dreamed what news the morrow's sun would see.

"Oh, my sheep!" groaned many a poor farmer.

"Oh, my Burgundy!" groaned Sir Godfrey.

"In that case," exclaimed Elaine, her cheeks pink with excitement, "I shall try the virtue of the legend, at any rate."

"Most impious, my daughter, most impious will such conduct be in the sight of Mother Church," said Father Anselm.

"Hear me, all people!" shouted Sir Godfrey, foreseeing that before the next Crusade came every drop of wine in his cellar would be swallowed by the Dragon; "hear me proclaim and solemnly promise: legend true or legend false, my daughter shall not face this risk. But if her heart go with it, her hand shall be given to that man who by night or light brings me this Dragon, alive or dead!"

"A useless promise, Sir Godfrey!" said Father Anselm, shrugging his shoulders. "We dare not discredit the word of thy respected grandsire."

"My respected grandsire be——"

"*What?*" said the Abbot.

"Became a credit to his family," said the Baron, quite mildly; "and I slight no word of his. But he did not contradict this legend in the vision, I think."

"No, he did not, papa," Miss Elaine put in. "He only mentioned another way of getting rid of this horrible Dragon. Now, papa, whatever you may say about—about my heart and hand," she continued, firmly, "I am going to meet the Monster alone myself, to-night."

"That you shall not," said Sir Godfrey.

"A hundred times no!" said a new voice from the crowd. "I will meet him myself!"

Geoffrey replyeth with deplorable Flippancy to Father Anselm.

All turned and saw a knight pushing his way through the people.

"Who are you?" inquired the Baron.

The stranger bowed haughtily; and Elaine watched him remove his helmet, and reveal underneath it the countenance of a young man who turned to her, and——

Why, what's this, Elaine? Why does everything seem to swim and grow misty as his eye meets yours? And why does he look at you so, and deeply flush to the very rim of his curly hair? And as his glance grows steadier and more intent upon your eyes that keep stealing over at him, can you imagine why his hand trembles on the hilt of his sword? Don't you remember what the legend said?

"Who are you?" the Baron repeated, impatiently.

"I am Geoffrey, son of Bertram of Poictiers," answered the young man.

"And what," asked Father Anselm, with a certain irony in his voice, "does Geoffrey, son of Bertram of Poictiers, so far away from his papa in this inclement weather?"

The knight surveyed the monk for a moment, and then said, "As thou art not my particular Father Confessor, stick to those matters which concern thee."

This reply did not please any man present, for it seemed to savour of disrespect. But Elaine lost no chance of watching the

youth, who now stood alone in the middle of the hall. Sir Francis
detected this, and smiled with a sly smile.

"Will some person inquire of this polite young man," he said,
"what he wishes with us?"

"Show me where this Dragon of Wantley comes," said Geoffrey, "for I intend to slay him to-night."

"Indeed, sir," fluttered Elaine, stepping towards him a little,
"I hope—that is, I beg you'll do no such dangerous thing as that
for my sake."

"For your sake?" Father Anselm broke in. "For your sake?
And why so? What should Elaine, daughter of Sir Godfrey
Disseisin, care for the carcase of Geoffrey, son of Bertram of
Poictiers?"

But Elaine, finding nothing to answer, turned rosy pink
instead.

"That rules you out!" exclaimed the Father, in triumph. "Your
legend demands a maid who never has cared for any man."

"Pooh!" said Geoffrey, "leave it to me."

"Seize him!" shouted Sir Godfrey in a rage. "He had ruled
out my daughter." Consistency had never been one of the Baron's
strong points.

"Seize him!" said Father Anselm. "He outrages Mother
Church."

The vassals closed up behind young Geoffrey, who was pinioned
in a second. He struggled with them till the veins stood out in
his forehead in blue knots; but, after all, one young man of
twenty is not much among a band of stout yeomen; and they all
fell in a heap on the floor, pulling and tugging at Geoffrey, who
had blacked several eyes, and done in a general way as much
damage as he possibly could under the circumstances.

But Elaine noticed one singular occurrence. Not a monk had
moved to seize the young man, except one, who rushed forward,

and was stopped, as though struck to stone, by Father Anselm's saying to him in a terrible undertone, "Hubert!"

Simply that word, spoken quickly; but not before this Hubert had brushed against her so that she was aware that there was something very hard and metallic underneath his gray gown. She betrayed no sign of knowledge or surprise on her face, however, but affected to be absorbed wholly in the fortunes of young Geoffrey, whom she saw collared and summarily put into a cage-like prison whose front was thick iron bars, and whose depth was in the vast outer wall of the Monastery, with a little window at the rear, covered with snow. The spring-lock of the gate shut upon him.

"And now," said Father Anselm, as the Monastery bell sounded once more, "if our guests will follow us, the mid-day meal awaits us below. We will deal with this hot-head later," he added, pointing to the prisoner.

So they slowly went out, leaving Geoffrey alone with his thoughts.

CHAPTER·VI

DOWN stairs the Grace was said, and the company was soon seated and ready for their mid-day meal.

"Our fare," said Father Anselm pleasantly to Sir Godfrey, who sat on his right, "is plain, but substantial."

"Oh—ah, very likely," replied the Baron, as he received a wooden basin of black-bean broth.

"Our drink is——"

The Baron lifted his eye hopefully.

"——remarkably pure water," Father Anselm continued. "Clement!" he called to the monk whose turn it was that day to hand the dishes, "Clement, a goblet of our well-water for Sir Godfrey Disseisin. One of the large goblets, Clement. We are indeed favoured, Baron, in having such a pure spring in the midst of our home."

"Oh—ah!" observed the Baron again, and politely nerved himself for a swallow. But his thoughts were far away in his own cellar over at Wantley, contemplating the casks whose precious gallons the Dragon had consumed. Could it be the strength of his imagination, or else why was it that through the chilling, unwelcome liquid he was now drinking he seemed to detect a lurking flavour of the very wine those casks had contained, his favourite Malvoisie?

Father Anselm noticed the same taste in his own cup, and did

not set it down to imagination, but afterwards sentenced Brother
Clement to bread and water during three days, for carelessness in
not washing the Monastery table-service more thoroughly.

"This simple food keeps you in beautiful health, Father," said
Mistletoe, ogling the swarthy face of the Abbot with an affection
that he duly noted.

"My daughter," he replied, gravely, "bodily infirmity is the
reward of the glutton. I am well, thank you."

Meanwhile, Elaine did not eat much. Her thoughts were busy,
and hurrying over recent events. Perhaps you think she lost her
heart in the last Chapter, and cannot lose it in this one unless it
is given back to her. But I do not agree with you; and I am
certain that, if you suggested such a notion to her, she would
become quite angry, and tell you not to talk such foolish nonsense.
People are so absurd about hearts, and all that sort of thing! No:
I do not really think she has lost her heart yet; but as she sits at
table these are the things she is feeling:

1. Not at all hungry.

2. Not at all thirsty.

3. What a hateful person that Father Anselm is!

4. Poor, poor young man!

5. Not that she thinks of him in *that* way, of course. The
idea! Horrid Father Anselm!

6. Any girl at all—no, not girl, *anybody* at all—who had human
justice would feel exactly as she did about the whole matter.

7. He was very good-looking, too.

8. Did he have—yes, they were blue. Very, very dark blue.

9. And a moustache? Well, yes.

Here she laughed, but no one noticed her idling with her
spoon. Then her eyes filled with tears, and she pretended to be
absorbed with the black-bean broth, though, as a matter of fact,
she did not see it in the least.

10. Why had he come there at all?

11. It was a perfect shame, treating him so.

12. Perhaps they were not blue, after all. But, oh! what a beautiful sparkle was in them!

After this, she hated Father Anselm worse than ever. And the more she hated him, the more some very restless delicious something made her draw long breaths. She positively must go up-stairs and see what He was doing and what He really looked like. This curiosity seized hold of her and set her thinking of some way to slip away unseen. The chance came through all present becoming deeply absorbed in what Sir Godfrey was saying to Father Anselm.

" Such a low, coarse, untaught brute as a dragon," he explained, " cannot possibly distinguish good wine from bad."

" Of a surety, no!" responded the monk.

" You agree with me upon that point?" said the Baron.

" Most certainly. Proceed."

" Well, I'm going to see that he gets nothing but the cider and small beer after this."

" But how will you prevent him, if he visit your cellar again?" Father Anselm inquired.

" I shall change all the labels, in the first place," the Baron answered.

" Ha! vastly well conceived," said Father Anselm. " You will label your Burgundy as if it were beer."

" And next," continued Sir Godfrey. " I shall shift the present positions of the hogsheads. That I shall do to-day, after relabelling. In the northern corner of the first wine vault I shall——"

Just as he reached this point, it was quite wonderful how strict an attention every monk paid to his words. They leaned forward, forgetting their dinner, and listened with all their might. One of them, who had evidently received an education, took notes under-

The Baron setteth forth his Plan for circumuenting the Dragon

neath the table. Thus it was that Elaine escaped observation when she left the refectory.

As she came up-stairs into the hall where Geoffrey was caged, she stepped lightly and kept where she could not be seen by him. All was quiet when she entered; but suddenly she heard the iron bars of the cage begin to rattle and shake, and at the same time Geoffrey's voice broke out in rage.

"I'll twist you loose," he said, "you—(rattle, shake)—you—(kick, bang)——" And here the shocking young man used words so violent and wicked that Elaine put her hands tight over her ears. "Why, he is just as dreadful as papa, just exactly!" she exclaimed to herself. "Whoever would have thought that that

angelic face—but I suppose they are all like that sometimes."
And she took her hands away again.

"Yes, I will twist you loose," he was growling hoarsely, while
the kicks and wrenches grew fiercer than ever, "or twist myself
stark, staring blind—and——"

"Oh, sir!" she said, running out in front of the cage.

He stopped at once, and stood looking at her. His breast-
plate and gauntlets were down on the floor, so his muscles might
have more easy play in dealing with the bars. Elaine noticed that
the youth's shirt was of very costly Eastern silk.

"I was thinking of getting out," he said at length, still standing
and looking at her.

"I thought I might—that is—you might——" began Miss Elaine,
and stopped. Upon which another silence followed.

"Lady, who sent you here?" he inquired.

"Oh, they don't know!" she replied, hastily; and then, seeing
how bright his face became, and hearing her own words, she
looked down, and the crimson went over her cheeks as he watched
her.

"Oh, if I could get out!" he said, desperately. "Lady, what
is your name, if I might be so bold."

"My name, sir, is Elaine. Perhaps there is a key somewhere,"
she said.

"And I am called Geoffrey," he said, in reply.

"I think we might find a key." Elaine repeated.

She turned towards the other side of the room, and there
hung a great bunch of brass keys dangling from the lock of a
heavy door.

Ah, Hubert! thou art more careless than Brother Clement, I
think, to have left those keys in such a place!

Quickly did Elaine cross to that closed door, and laid her
hand upon the bunch. The door came open the next moment,

and she gave a shriek to see the skin of a huge lizard-beast fall
forward at her feet, and also many cups and flagons, that rolled
over the floor, dotting it with little drops of wine.

Hearing Elaine shriek, and not able to see from his prison
what had befallen her, Geoffrey shouted out in terror to know if
she had come to any hurt.

"No," she told him; and stood eyeing first the crocodile's hide
and then the cups, setting her lips together very firmly. "And
they were not even dry," she said after a while. For she began
to guess a little of the truth.

"Not dry? Who?" inquired Geoffrey.

"Oh, Geoffrey!" she burst out in deep anger, and then
stopped, bewildered. But his heart leaped to hear her call his
name.

"Are there no keys?" he asked.

"Keys? Yes!" she cried, and, running with them back to the
bars, began trying one after another in trembling haste till the
lock clicked pleasantly, and out marched young Geoffrey.

Now what do you suppose this young man did when he found
himself free once more, and standing close by the lovely young
person to whom he owed his liberty? Did he place his heels
together, and let his arms hang gracefully, and so bow with respect
and a manner at once dignified and urbane, and say, "Miss Elaine,
permit me to thank you for being so kind as to let me out of
prison?" That is what he ought to have done, of course, if he
had known how to conduct himself like a well-brought-up young
man. But I am sorry to have to tell you that Geoffrey did nothing of the sort, but, instead of that, behaved in a most outrageous
manner. He did not thank her at all. He did not say one single
word to her. He simply put one arm round her waist and gave
her a kiss!

"Geoffrey!" she murmured, "don't!"

But Geoffrey did, with the most astonishing and complacent disobedience.

"Oh, Geoffrey!" she whispered, looking the other way, "how wrong of you! And of me!" she added a little more softly still, escaping from him suddenly, and facing about.

"I don't see that," said Geoffrey. "I love you, Elaine. Elaine, darling, I——"

"Oh, but you mustn't!" answered she, stepping back as he came nearer.

This was simply frightful! And so sudden. To think of her —Elaine!—but she couldn't think at all. Happy? Why, how wicked! How had she ever——

"No, you must not," she repeated, and backed away still farther.

"But I will!" said this lover, quite loudly, and sprang so quickly to where she stood that she was in his arms again, and this time without the faintest chance of getting out of them until he should choose to free her.

It was no use to struggle now, and she was still, like some wild bird. But she knew that she was really his, and was glad of it. And she looked up at him and said, very softly, "Geoffrey, we are wasting time."

"Oh, no, not at all," said Geoffrey.

"But we are."

"Say that you love me."

"But haven't I—ah, Geoffrey, please don't begin again."

"Say that you love me."

She did.

Then, taking his hand, she led him to the door she had opened. He stared at the crocodile, at the wine-cups, and then he picked up a sheet of iron and a metal torch.

"I suppose it is their museum," he said; "don't you?"

"Their museum! Geoffrey, think a little."

"They seem to keep very good wine," he remarked, after smelling at the demijohn.

"Don't you see? Can't you understand?" she said.

"No, not a bit. What's that thing, do you suppose?" he added, giving the crocodile a kick.

"Oh, me, but men are simple, men are simple!" said Elaine, in despair. "Geoffrey, listen! That wine is my father's wine, from his own cellar. There is none like it in all England."

"Then I don't see why he gave it to a parcel of monks," replied the young man.

Elaine clasped her hands in hopelessness, gave him a kiss, and became mistress of the situation.

"Now, Geoffrey," she said, "I will tell you what you and I have really found out." Then she quickly recalled all the recent events. How her father's cellar had been broken into; how Mistletoe had been chained to a rock for a week and no dragon had come near her. She bade him remember how just now Father Anselm had opposed every plan for meeting the Dragon, and at last she pointed to the crocodile.

"Ha!" said Geoffrey, after thinking for a space. "Then you mean——."

"Of course I do," she interrupted. "The Dragon of Wantley is now down-stairs with papa eating dinner, and pretending he never drinks anything stronger than water. What do you say to that, sir?"

"This is a foul thing!" cried the knight. "Here have I been damnably duped. Here——" but speech deserted him. He glared at the crocodile with a bursting countenance, then drove his toe against it with such vigour that it sailed like a foot-ball to the farther end of the hall.

"Papa has been duped, and everybody," said Elaine. "Papa's French wine——"

Geoffrey tuggeth at the Bars

"They swore to me in Flanders I should find a real dragon here," he continued, raging up and down, and giving to the young lady no part of his attention. She began to fear he was not thinking of her.

"Geoffrey——" she ventured.

"They swore it. They had invited me to hunt a dragon with them in Flanders,—Count Faux Pas and his Walloons. We hunted day and night, and the quest was barren. They then directed me to this island of Britain, in which they declared a dragon might be found by any man who so desired. They lied in their throats. I have come leagues for nothing." Here he looked viciously at the distant hide of the crocodile. "But I shall slay the monk," he added. "A masquerading caitiff! Lying varlets! And all for nothing! The monk shall die, however."

"Have you come for nothing, Geoffrey?" murmured Elaine.

"Three years have I been seeking dragons in all countries, chasing deceit over land and sea. And now once more my dearest hope falls empty and stale. Why, what's this?" A choking sound beside him stopped the flow of his complaints.

"Oh, Geoffrey,—oh, miserable me!" The young lady was dissolved in tears.

"Elaine—dearest—don't."

"You said you had come for n—nothing, and it was all st—stale."

"Ha, I am a fool, indeed! But it was the Dragon, dearest. I had made so sure of an honest one in this adventure."

"Oh, oh!" went Miss Elaine, with her head against his shoulder.

"There, there! You're sweeter than all the dragons in the world, my little girl," said he. And although this does not appear to be a great compliment, it comforted her wonderfully in the end; for he said it in her ear several times without taking his lips away. "Yes," he continued, "I was a fool. By your father's own word you're mine. I have caught the Dragon. Come, my girl! We'll down to the refectory forthwith and denounce him."

With this, he seized Elaine's hand and hastily made for the stairs.

"But hold, Geoffrey, hold! Oh—I am driven to act not as maidens should," sighed Elaine. "He it is who ought to do the thinking. But, dear me! he does not know how. Do you not see we should both be lost, were you to try any such wild plan?"

"Not at all. Your father would give you to me."

"Oh, no, no, Geoffrey; indeed, papa would not. His promise was about a dragon. A live or a dead dragon must be brought to him. Even if he believed you now, even if that dreadful Father Anselm could not invent some lie to put us in the wrong, you and I could never—that is—papa would not feel bound by his promise simply because you did that. There must be a dragon somehow."

"How can there be a dragon if there is not a dragon?" asked Geoffrey.

"Wait, wait, Geoffrey! Oh, how can I think of everything all at once?" and Elaine pressed her hands to her temples.

"Darling," said the knight, with his arms once more around her, "let us fly now."

"Now? They would catch us at once."

"Catch us! not they! with my sword——"

"Now, Geoffrey, of course you are brave. But do be sensible. You are only one. No! I won't even argue such nonsense. They must never know about what we have been doing up here; and you must go back into that cage at once."

"What, and be locked up, and perhaps murdered to-night, and never see your face again?"

"But you shall see me again, and soon. That is what I am thinking about."

"How can you come in here, Elaine?"

"You must come to me. I have it! To-night, at half-past eleven, come to the cellar-door at the Manor, and I will be there to let you in. Then we can talk over everything quietly. I have no time to think now."

"The cellar! at the Manor! And how, pray, shall I get out of that cage?"

"Cannot you jump from the little window at the back?"

Geoffrey ran in to see. "No," he said, returning; "it is many spans from the earth."

Elaine had hurried into the closet, whence she returned with a dusty coil of rope. "Here, Geoffrey; quickly! put it about your waist. Wind it so. But how clumsy you are!"

He stood smiling down at her, and she very deftly wound the cord up and down, over and over his body, until its whole length lay comfortably upon him.

"Now, your breast-plate, quick!"

She helped him put his armour on again; and, as they were

engaged at that, singing voices came up the stairs from the distant
dining-hall.

"The Grace." she exclaimed ; "they will be here in a moment."

Geoffrey took a last kiss, and bolted into his cage. She, with
the keys, made great haste to push the crocodile and other objects
once more into their hiding-place. Cups and flagons and all rattled
back without regard to order, as they had already been flung not
two hours before. The closet-door shut, and Elaine hung the keys
from the lock as she had found them.

"Half-past eleven," she said to Geoffrey, as she ran by his cage
towards the stairs.

"One more, darling,—please, one ! through the bars !" he be-
sought her, in a voice so tender, that for my part I do not see how
she had the heart to refuse him. But she continued her way, and
swiftly descending the stairs was found by the company, as they
came from the hall, busily engaged in making passes with Sir
Godfrey's sword, which he had left leaning near the door.

"A warlike daughter, Sir Godfrey !" said Father Anselm.

"Ah, if I were a man to go on a Crusade !" sighed Miss
Elaine.

"Hast thou, my daughter." said Father Anselm, "thought better
of thy rash intentions concerning this Dragon ?"

"I am travelling towards better thoughts, Father," she answered.

But Sir Francis did not wholly believe the young lady ; and
was not at rest until Sir Godfrey assured him her good conduct
should be no matter of her own choosing.

"You see," insinuated the Abbot, "so sweet a maid as yours
would be a treat for the unholy beast. A meal like that would
incline him to remain in a neighbourhood where such dainties were
to be found."

"I'll have no legends and fool's tricks." exclaimed the Baron.
"She shall be locked in her room to-night."

"Not if she can help it," thought Miss Elaine. Her father had imprudently spoken too loud.

"'Twere a wise precaution," murmured Father Anselm. "What are all the vintages of this earth by the side of a loving daughter?"

"Quite so, quite so!" Sir Godfrey assented. "Don't you think," he added, wistfully, "that another Crusade may come along soon?"

"Ah, my son, who can say? Tribulation is our meted heritage. Were thy thoughts more high, the going of thy liquors would not cause thee such sorrow. Learn to enjoy the pure cold water."

"Good-afternoon," said the Baron.

When all the guests had departed and the door was shut safe behind them, the Father and his holy companions broke into loud mirth. "The Malvoisie is drunk up," said they; "to-night we'll pay his lordship's cellars another visit."

T O have steered a sudden course among dangerous rocks and rapids and come safe through, puts in the breast of the helmsman a calm content with himself, for which no man will blame him. What in this world is there so lifts one into complacency as the doing of a bold and cool-headed thing? Let the helmsman sleep sound when he has got to land! But if his content overtake him still on the water, so that he grows blind to the treacherous currents that eddy where all looks placid to the careless eye, let him beware!

Sir Francis came in front of the cage where sat young Geoffrey inside, on the floor. The knight had put his head down between his knees, and seemed doleful enough.

"Aha!" thought Sir Francis, giving the motionless figure a dark look, "my hawk is moulting. We need scarcely put a hood on such a tersel."

Next he looked at the shut door of the closet, and a shaft of alarm shot through him to see the keys hanging for anybody to make use of them that pleased. He thought of Elaine, and her leaving the table without his seeing her go. What if she had paid this room a visit?

"Perhaps that bird with head under wing in there," he mused, looking once more at Geoffrey, "is not the simple-witted nestling he looks. My son!" he called.

But the youth did not care to talk, and so showed no sign.

"My son, peace be with you!" repeated Father Anselm, coming to the bars and wearing a benevolent mien.

Geoffrey remained quite still.

"If repentance for thy presumption hath visited thee——" went on the Father.

"Hypocrite!" was the word that jumped to the youth's lips; but fortunately he stopped in time, and only moved his legs with some impatience.

"I perceive with pain, my son," said Father Anselm, "that repentance hath not yet visited thee. Well, 'twill come. And that's a blessing too," he added, sighing very piously.

"He plays a part pretty well," thought Geoffrey as he listened. "So will I." Then he raised his head.

"How long am I to stay in this place?" he inquired, taking a tone of sullen humour, such as he thought would fit a prisoner.

"Certainly until thy present unbridled state of sin is purged out of thee," replied the Father.

"Under such a dose as thou art," Geoffrey remarked, "that will be soon."

"This is vain talk, my son," said the Abbot. "Were I of the children of this world, my righteous indignation——"

"Pooh!" said Geoffrey.

"—— would light on thee heavily. But we who have renounced the world and its rottenness" (here his voice fell into a manner of chanting) "make a holiday of forgiving injuries, and find a pleasure even in pain."

"Open this door then," Geoffrey answered, "and I'll provide thee with a whole week of joy."

"Nay," said Father Anselm, "I had never gathered from thy face that thou wert such a knave."

"At least in the matter of countenances I have the advantage of thee," the youth observed.

"I perceive," continued the Father, "that I must instruct thy spirit in many things,—submission, among others. Therefore thou shalt bide with us for a month or two."

"That I'll not!" shouted Geoffrey, forgetting his rôle of prisoner.

"She cannot unlock thee," Father Anselm said, with much art slipping Elaine into the discourse.

Geoffrey glared at the Abbot, who now hoped to lay a trap for him by means of his temper. So he went further in the same direction. "Her words are vainer than most women's," he said; "though a lover would trust in them, of course."

The knight swelled in his rage, and might have made I know not what unsafe rejoinder; but the cords that Elaine had wound about him naturally tightened as he puffed out, and seemed by their pressure to check his speech and bid him be wary. So he changed his note, and said haughtily, "Because thy cowl and thy gown shield thee, presume not to speak of one whose cause I took up in thy presence, and who is as high above thee in truth as she is in every other quality and virtue."

"This callow talk, my son," said the Abbot quietly, "wearies me much. Lay thee down and sleep thy sulks off, if thou art able." Upon this, he turned away to the closet where hung the brass keys, and opened the door a-crack. He saw the hide of the crocodile leaning against it, and the overturned cups. "Just as that boy Hubert packed them," he thought to himself in satisfaction; "no one has been prying here. I flatter myself upon a skilful morning's work. I have knocked the legend out of the Baron's head. He'll see to it the girl keeps away. And as for yon impudent witling in the cage, we shall transport him beyond the seas, if convenient; if not, a knife in his gullet will make him forget the Dragon of Wantley. Truly, I am master of the situation!" And

as his self-esteem grew, the Grand Marshal rubbed his hands, and
went out of the hall, too much pleased with himself to notice certain little drops of wine dotted here and there close by the closet,
and not yet quite dry, which, had his eye fallen upon them, might
have set him a-thinking.

So Geoffrey was left in his prison to whatever comfort meditation might bring him; and the monks of Oyster-le-Main took off
their gowns, and made themselves ready for another visit to the
wine-cellars of Wantley Manor.

The day before Christmas came bleakly to its end over dingle
and fen, and the last gray light died away. Yet still you could
hear the hissing snow beat down through the bramble-thorn and
the dry leaves. After evening was altogether set in, Hubert
brought the knight a supper that was not a meal a hungry man
might be over joyful at seeing; yet had Hubert (in a sort of
fellowship towards one who seemed scarcely longer seasoned in
manhood than himself, and whom he had seen blacken eyes in a
very valiant manner) secretly prepared much better food than had
been directed by his worship the Abbot.

The prisoner feigned sleep, and started up at the rattle which
the plate made as it was set down under his bars.

"Is it morning?" he asked.

"Morning, forsooth!" Hubert answered. "Three more hours,
and we reach only midnight." And both young men (for different
reasons) wished in their hearts it were later.

"Thou speakest somewhat curtly for a friar," said Geoffrey.

"Alas, I am but a novice, brother," whined the minstrel, "and
fall easily back into my ancient and godless syntax. There is food.
Pax vobiscum, son of the flesh." Then Hubert went over to the
closet, and very quietly unlocking the door removed the crocodile
and the various other implements that were necessary in bringing
into being the dread Dragon of Wantley. He carried them away

to a remote quarter of the Monastery, where the Guild began
preparations that should terrify
any superstitious witness of their
journey to get the Baron's wine.
Geoffrey, solitary and watchful in
his chilly cage, knew what work
must be going on, and waited
his time in patience.

At supper over at Wantley
there was but slight inclination
to polite banter. Only the family Chaplain, mindful that this
was Christmas Eve, attempted to
make a little small talk with Sir
Godfrey.

"Christmas," he observed to
the Baron, "is undoubtedly coming."

As the Baron did not appear
to have any rejoinder to this, the young divine continued, pleasantly.

"Though indeed," he said, "we might make this assertion upon
any day of the three hundred and sixty-five, and (I think) remain
accurate."

"The celery," growled the Baron, looking into his plate.

"Quite so," cried the Chaplain, cheerily. He had failed to catch
the remark. "Though of course everything does depend on one's
point of view, after all."

"That celery, Whelpdale!" roared Sir Godfrey.

The terrified Buttons immediately dropped a large venison pasty
into Mrs. Mistletoe's lap. She, having been somewhat tried of late,
began screeching. Whelpdale caught up the celery, and blindly

rushed towards Sir Godfrey, while Popham, foreseeing trouble, rapidly ascended the sideboard. The Baron stepped out of Whelp-dale's path, and as he passed by administered so much additional speed that little Buttons flew under the curtained archway and down many painful steps into the scullery, and was not seen again during that evening.

When Sir Godfrey had reseated himself, it seemed to the Rev. Hucbald (such was the Chaplain's name) that the late interruption might be well smoothed over by conversation. So he again ad-dressed the Baron.

"To be sure," said he, taking a manner of sleek clerical pleasantry, "though we can so often say 'Christmas is coming.' I suppose that if at some suitable hour to-morrow afternoon I said to you, 'Christmas is going,' you would grant it to be a not inac-curate remark?" The Baron ate his dinner.

"I think so," pursued the Rev. Hucbald. "Yes. And by the way, I notice with pleasure that this snow, which falls so continually, makes the event of a green Christmas most improbable. Indeed, —of course the proverb is familiar to you?—the graveyards should certainly not be fat this season. I like a lean graveyard," smiled the Rev. Hucbald.

"I hate a —— fool!" exclaimed Sir Godfrey, angrily.

After this the family fell into silence. Sir Godfrey munched his food, brooding gloomily over his plundered wine-cellar; Mrs. Mis-tletoe allowed fancy to picture herself wedded to Father Anselm, if only he had not been a religious person; and Elaine's thoughts were hovering over the young man who sat in a cage till time came for him to steal out and come to her. But the young lady was wonderfully wise, nevertheless.

"Papa," she said, as they left the banquet-hall, "if it is about me you're thinking, do not be anxious any more at all."

"Well, well; what's the matter now?" said the Baron.

"Papa, dear," began Elaine, winsomely pulling at a tassel on his dining-coat, "do you know, I've been thinking."

"Think some more, then," he replied. "It will come easier when you're less new at it."

"Now, papa! just when I've come to say—when I want—when you—it's very hard——" and here the artful minx could proceed no further, but turned a pair of shining eyes at him, and then looked the other way, blinking rapidly.

"Oh, good Lord!" muttered Sir Godfrey, staring hard at the wall.

"Papa—it's about the Dragon—and I've been wrong. Very wrong. Yes; I know I have. I was foolish." She was silent again. Was she going to cry, after all? The Baron shot a nervous glance at her from the corner of his eye. Then he said, "Hum!" He hoped very fervently there were to be no tears. He desired to remain in a rage, and lock his daughter up, and not put anything into her stocking this Christmas Eve; and here she was, threatening to be sorry for the past, and good for the future, and everything a parent could wish. Never mind. You can't expect to get off as easily as all that. She had been very outrageous. Now he would be dignified and firm.

"Of course I should obey Father Anselm," she continued.

"You should obey me," said Sir Godfrey.

"And I do hope another Crusade will come soon. Don't you think they might have one, papa? How happy I shall be when your wine is safe from that horrid Dragon!"

"Don't speak of that monster!" shouted the Baron, forgetting all about firmness and dignity. "Don't dare to allude to the reptile in my presence. Look here!" He seized up a great jug labelled "Château Lafitte," and turned it upside down.

"Why, it's empty!" said Elaine.

"Ha!" snorted the Baron; "empty indeed." Then he set the

jug down wrong side up, and remained glaring at it fixedly, while
his chest rose and fell in deep heavings.

"Don't mind it so much, papa," said Elaine, coming up to him.
"This very next season will Mistletoe and I brew a double quantity
of cowslip wine."

"Brrrrooo!" went Sir Godfrey, with a shiver.

"And I'm sure they'll have another Crusade soon; and then
my brother Roland can go, and the Drag— and the curse will be
removed. Of course, I know that is the only way to get rid of it,
if Father Anselm said so. I was very foolish and wrong. Indeed
I was," said she, and looked up in his face with eyes where shone
such dear, good, sweet, innocent, daughterly affection, that nobody in
the wide world could have suspected she was thinking as hard as
she could think, "If only he won't lock me up! if only he won't!
But, oh, it's dreadful in me to be deceiving him so!"

"There, there!" said the Baron, and cleared his throat. Then
he kissed her. Where were firmness and dignity now?

He let her push him into the chimney-corner, and down into a
seat; and then what did this sly, shocking girl do but sit on his
knee and tell him nobody ever had such a papa before, and she
could never possibly love any one half so much as she loved him,
and weren't he and she going to have a merry Christmas to-
morrow?

"How about that pretty young man? Hey? What?" said Sir
Godfrey, in high good-humour.

"Who?" snapped Elaine.

"I think this girl knows," he answered, adopting a roguish
countenance.

"Oh, I suppose you mean that little fellow this morning.
Pooh!"

"Ho! ho!" said her father. "Ho! ho! Little fellow! He was
a pretty large fellow in somebody's eyes, I thought. What are

you so red about? Ho! ho!" and the Baron popped his own eyes
at her with vast relish.

"Really, papa," said Miss Elaine, rising from his knee, with much
coldness, "I hardly understand you, I think. If you find it amusing
(and you seem to) to pretend that I——" she said no more, but
gave a slight and admirable toss of the head. "And now I am
very sleepy," she added. "What hour is it?"

Sir Godfrey took out his grandfather's sun-dial, and held it to
the lamp. "Bless my soul," he exclaimed; "it's twenty-two
o'clock." (That's ten at night nowadays, young people, and much
too late for you to be down-stairs, any of you.)

"Get to your bed at once," continued Sir Godfrey, "or
you'll never be dressed in time for Chapel on Christmas morning."

So Elaine went to her room, and took off her clothes, and hung
up her stocking at the foot of the bed. Did she go to sleep?
Not she. She laid with eyes and ears wide open. And now alone
here in the dark, where she had nothing to do but wait, she found
her heart beating in answer to her anxious and expectant thoughts.
She heard the wind come blustering from far off across the silent
country. Then a snore from Mistletoe in the next room made her
jump. Twice a bar of moonlight fell along the floor, wavering and
weak, then sank out, and the pat of the snow-flakes began again.
After a while came a step through the halls to her door, and
stopped. She could scarcely listen, so hard she was breathing.
Was her father going to turn the key in her door, after all? No
such thought was any longer in his mind. She shut her eyes
quickly as he entered. His candle shone upon her quiet head, that
was nearly buried out of sight; then laughter shook him to see the
stocking, and he went softly out. He had put on his bed-room
slippers; but, as he intended to make a visit to the cellar before
retiring, it seemed a prudent thing to wear his steel breastplate;

GEOFFREY·GOETH·TO·MEET·THE·DRAGON

and over this he had slipped his quilted red silk dressing-gown, for it was a very cold night.

Was there a sound away off somewhere out-of-doors? No. He descended heavily through the sleeping house. When the candle burned upright and clear yellow, his gait was steady; but he started many times at corners where its flame bobbed and flattened and shrunk to a blue, sickly rag half torn from the wick. "Ouf! Mort d'aieul!" he would mutter. "But I must count my wine to-night." And so he came down into the wide cellars, and trod tiptoe among the big round tuns. With a wooden mallet he tapped them, and shook his head to hear the hollow humming that their emptiness gave forth. No oath came from him at all, for the matter was too grievous. The darkness that filled everywhere save just next to the candle, pressed harder and harder upon him. He looked at the door which led from inside here out into the night, and it was comfortable to know how thick were the panels and how stout the bolts and hinges.

"I can hold my own against any man, and have jousted fairly in my time," he thought to himself, and touched his sword. "But —um!" The notion of meeting a fiery dragon in combat spoke loudly to the better part of his valour. Suddenly a great rat crossed his foot. Ice and fire went from his stomach all through him, and he sprang on a wooden stool, and then found he was shaking. Soon he got down, with sweaty hands.

"Am I getting a coward?" he asked aloud. He seized the mallet that had fallen, and struck a good knock against the nearest hogshead. Ah—ha! This one, at least, was full. He twisted the wooden stop and drank what came, from the hollow of his hand. It was cowslip wine. Ragingly he spluttered and gulped, and then kicked the bins with all his might. While he was stooping to rub his toe, who should march in but Miss Elaine, dressed and ready for young Geoffrey. But she caught sight of her father in time, and stepped back into the passage in a flutter. Good heavens! This would never do. Geoffrey might be knocking at the cellar-door at any moment. Her papa must be got away at once.

"Papa! papa!" she cried, running in.

Sir Godfrey sprang into the air, throwing mallet and candle against the wine-butts. Then he saw it was only his daughter.

"Wretched girl! you—you—if you don't want to become an orphan, never tamper like that with my nerves again in your life. What are you come here for? How dare you leave your bed at such an hour?"

"Oh, mercy forgive us!" whimpered a new voice.

There was Mistletoe at the door of the passage, a candle lifted high above her head and wobbling, so that it shook the grease all over her night-cap. With the other hand she clutched her cami-sole, while beneath a yellow flannel petticoat her fat feet were rocking in the raw-wool foot-mittens she wore.

"Oh, dear: oh, Sir Godfrey! Oh, me!" said she.

"Saint Charity! What do you want? Holy Ragbag, what's the matter? Is everybody in my house going stark mad?" Here the Baron fell over the stool in the dark. "Give me my candle!"

7

he roared. "Light my candle! What business have either of you to come here?"

"Please, sir, it's Miss Elaine I came for. Oh, me! I'll catch my death of cold. Her door shutting waked me up-stairs. Oh, dear! Where are we coming to?"

"You old mattrass!" said Sir Godfrey. Then he turned to his daughter. But this young lady had had a little time to gather her thoughts in. So she cut short all awkward questionings with excellent promptness.

"Papa!" she began, breathlessly. "There! I heard it again!"

"Heard it? What?" cried the Baron, his eyes starting.

"It waked me up-stairs, and I ran to get you in your room, and you——"

"It—it? What's it? What waked you?" broke in Sir Godfrey, his voice rising to a shriek.

"There it is again!" exclaimed Elaine, clasping her hands. "He's coming! I hear him. The Dragon! Oh!"

With this, she pretended to rush for the passage, where the squeaks of Mistletoe could be heard already growing distant in the house. Away bolted Sir Godfrey after her, shouting to Elaine in terror undisguised, "Lock your door! Lock your door!" as he fled up-stairs.

So there stood Miss Elaine alone, with the coast clear, and no danger from these two courageous guardians. Then came a knock from outside, and her heart bounded as she ran through the cellar and undid the door.

"You darling!" said Geoffrey, jumping in with legs all covered with snow. He left the door open wide, and had taken four or five kisses at the least before she could stop him. "The moon was out for a while," he continued, "and the snow stopped. So I came a long way roundabout, that my tracks should not be seen. That's good strategy."

But this strange young lady said no word, and looked at him as if she were going to cry.

"Why, what's the matter, dear?" he asked.

"Oh, Geoffrey! I have been deceiving papa so."

"Pooh! It's not to be thought of."

"But I can't help thinking. I never supposed I could do so. And it comes so terribly easy. And I'm not a bit clever when I'm good. And—oh!" She covered her face and turned away from him.

"Stuff and nonsense!" Geoffrey broke out. "Do be reasonable. Here is a dragon. Isn't there?"

"Yes."

"And everybody wants to get rid of him?"

"Yes."

"And he's robbing your father?"

"Yes."

"So you're acting for your father's good."

"Y—yes."

"Then——"

"Now, Geoffrey, all your talking doesn't hide the badness in the least bit."

She was silent again; then suddenly seemed greatly relieved. "I don't care," she declared. "Papa locked me up for a whole week, when all I wanted was to help him and everybody get rid of the Dragon. And I am too old to be treated so. And now I am just going to pretend there's a dragon when there's not. Oh, what's that?"

This time it was no sham. Faint and far from the direction of Oyster-le-Main came the roar of the Dragon of Wantley over fields and farms.

CHAPTER·VIII

UN instantly into the house," said Geoffrey to Elaine, and he dragged out his sword.

But she stared at him, and nothing further.

"Or no. Stay here and see me kill him," the boy added, pridefully.

"Kill him!" said she, in amazement. "Do you suppose that papa, with all his experience, couldn't tell it was an imitation dragon? And you talk of strategy! I have thought much about to-night,— and, Geoffrey, you must do just the thing that I bid you, and nothing else. Promise."

"I think we'll hear first what your wisdom is," said he, shaking his head like the sage youth that he was.

"Promise!" she repeated, "else I go away at once, and leave you. Now! One—two—thrrr——"

"I promise!" he shouted.

"'Sh! Papa's window is just round the tower. Now, sir, you must go over yonder within those trees."

"Where?"

"There where the snow has dipped the branches low down. And leave me alone in the cellar with the Dragon."

"With the Dragon? Alone? I did not know you counted me a lunatic," replied Geoffrey. Then, after a look over the fields where the storm was swirling, he gave attention to the point of his sword.

"Where's your promise?" said she. "Will you break your word so soon?"

A big gust of wind flung the snow sharp against their faces.

"Did you expect——" began the young knight, and then said some words that I suppose gentlemen in those old times were more prone to use before ladies than they are to-day. Which shows the optimists are right.

Then, still distant, but not so distant, came another roar.

"Geoffrey!" Elaine said, laying a hand upon his arm; "indeed, you must hear me now, and make no delay with contrary notions. There is no danger for me. Look. He will first be by himself to clear the way of watchers. No one peeps out of windows when the Dragon's howling. Next, the rest will come and all go into papa's cellar for the wine. But we must get these others away, and that's for you." She paused.

"Well? Well?" he said.

"It will go thus: the passage shall hide me, and the door of it be shut. You'll watch over by the trees, and when you see all have come inside here, make some sort of noise at the edge of the wood."

"What sort of noise?"

"Oh,—not as if you suspected. Seem to be passing by. Play you are a villager going home late. When they hear that, they'll run away for fear of their secret. The Dragon will surely stay behind."

"Why will he stay behind? Why will they run away?"

"Dear Geoffrey, don't you see that if these men were to be seen in company with the Dragon by one who till now knew them as monks, where would their living be gone to? Of course, they will get themselves out of sight, and the Dragon will remain as a sort of human scarecrow. Then I'll come out from the passage-door."

"One would almost think you desired that villain to kill you," said Geoffrey. "No, indeed. I'll not consent to that part."

"How shall he kill me here?" Elaine replied. "Do you not see the Dragon of Wantley would have to carry a maiden away? He would not dare to put me to the sword. When I come, I shall speak three words to him. Before there is time for him to think what to do, you will hear me say (for you must have now run up from the wood) 'the legend has come true!' Then, when I tell him that, do you walk in ready with your sword to keep him polite. Oh, indeed," said the lady, with her eyes sparkling on Geoffrey, "we must keep his manners good for him. For I think he's one of those persons who might turn out very rude in a trying situation."

All this was far from pleasing to young Geoffrey. But Elaine showed him how no other way was to be found by which Sir Francis could be trapped red-handed and distant from help. While the knight was bending his brows down with trying to set his thoughts into some order that should work out a better device, a glare shone over the next hill against the falling flakes.

"Quick!" said Elaine.

She withdrew into the cellar on the instant, and the great door closed between them. Geoffrey stood looking at it very anxiously, and then walked backwards, keeping close to the walls, and so round the tower and into the court, whence he turned and ploughed as fast as he could through the deep drifts till he was inside the trees. "If they spy my steps," he thought, "it will seem as though some one of the house had gone in there to secure the door."

Once more the glare flashed against the swiftly-descending curtains of the storm. Slowly it approached, sometimes illuminating a tree-trunk for a moment, then suddenly gleaming on the white mounds where rocks lay deeply cloaked.

"He is pretty slow," said Geoffrey, shifting the leg he was leaning on.

The Dragon thinketh to slake his thirst.

A black mass moved into sight, and from it came spoutings of fire that showed dark, jagged wings heavily flapping. It walked a little and stopped; then walked again. Geoffrey could see a great snout and head rocking and turning. Dismal and unspeakable sounds proceeded from the creature as it made towards the cellar-door. After it had got close and leaned against the panels in a toppling, swaying fashion, came a noise of creaking and fumbling, and then the door rolled aside upon its hinges. Next, the blurred white ridge towards Oyster-le-Main was darkened with moving specks that came steadily near; and man by man of the Guild reached the open door crouching, whispered a word or two, and crept inside. They made no sound that could be heard above the hissing of the downward flakes and the wind that moaned always, but louder sometimes. Only Elaine, with her ear to the cold iron key-hole of the passage-door, could mark the clink of armour, and shivered as she stood in the dark. And now the cellar is full,—but not of gray gowns. The candle flames show little glistening sparks in the black coats of mail, and the sight of themselves cased in steel, and each bearing an empty keg, stirred a laughter among them. Then the kegs were set down without noise on the earthy floor among the bins. The Dragon was standing on his crooked scaly hind-legs; and to see the grim, changeless jaw and eyes brought a dead feeling around the heart. But the two bungling fore-paws moved upwards, shaking like a machine, and out of a slit in the hide came two white hands that lifted to one side the brown knarled mask of the crocodile. There was the black head of Sir Francis Almoign. "'Tis hot in there," he said; and with two fingers he slung the drops of sweat from his forehead.

"Wet thy whistle before we begin," said Hubert, filling a jug for him. Sir Francis took it in both hands, and then clutched it tightly as a sudden singing was set up out in the night.

> " Come, take a wife,
> Come, take a wife,
> Ere thou learnest age's treasons!"

The tune came clear and jolly, cutting through the muffled noises of the tempest.

"Blood and death!" muttered Hubert.

Each figure had sprung into a stiff position of listening.

> " Quit thy roving ;
> Shalt by loving
> Not wax lean in stormy seasons.
> Ho! ho! oh,—ho!
> Not wax lean in——"

Here the strain snapped off short. Then a whining voice said, "Oh, I have fallen again! A curse on these roots. Lucifer fell only once, and 'twas enough for him. I have looked on the wine when it was red, and my dame Jeanie will know it soon, oh, soon! But my sober curse on these roots."

"That's nothing," said Hubert. "There's a band of Christmas singers has strolled into these parts to chant carols. One of them has stopped too long at the tavern."

"Do I see a light?" said the voice. "Help! Give me a light, and let me go home.

> "Quit thy roving:
> Shalt by loving——"

"Shall I open his throat, that he may sing the next verse in heaven?" Hubert inquired.

"No, fool!" said Sir Francis. "Who knows if his brother sots are not behind him to wake the house? This is too dangerous to-night. Away with you, every one. Stoop low till ye are well among the fields, and then to Oyster-le-Main! I'll be Dragon for a while, and follow after."

Quickly catching up his keg, each man left the cellar like a shadow. Geoffrey, from the edge of the wood, saw them come out and dissolve away into the night. With the tube of the torch at his lips, Sir Francis blew a blast of fire out at the door, then covered his head once more with the grinning crocodile. He roared twice, and heard something creak behind him, so turned to see what had made it. There was Miss Elaine on the passage-steps. Her lips moved to speak, but for a short instant fear put a silence upon her that she found no voice to break. He, with a notion she was there for the sake of the legend, waved his great paws and trundled towards where she was standing.

"Do not forget to roar, sir," said the young lady, managing her voice so there was scarce any tremble to be heard in it.

At this the Dragon stood still.

"You perceive," she said to him, "after all, a dragon, like a mouse, comes to the trap."

"Not quite yet," cried Sir Francis, in a terrible voice, and rushed upon her, meaning death.

"The legend has come true!" she loudly said.

A gleaming shaft of steel whistled across the sight of Sir Francis.

"Halt there!" thundered Geoffrey, leaping between the two, and poising his sword for a lunge.

"My hour has come," Sir Francis thought. For he was cased in the stiff hide, and could do nothing in defence.

"Now shalt thou lick the earth with thy lying tongue," said Geoffrey.

A sneer came through the gaping teeth of the crocodile.

"Valiant, indeed!" the voice said. "Very valiant and knightly, oh son of Bertram of Poictiers! Frenchmen know when to be bold. Ha! ha!"

"Crawl out of that nut, thou maggot," answered Geoffrey, "and taste thy doom."

Here was a chance, the gift of a fool. The two white hands appeared and shifted the mask aside, letting them see a cunning hope on his face.

"Do not go further, sir," said Elaine. "It is for the good of us all that you abide where you are. As I shall explain."

"What is this, Elaine?" said Geoffrey.

"Your promise!" she answered, lifting a finger at him.

There was a dry crack from the crocodile's hide.

"Villain!" cried Geoffrey, seizing the half-extricated body by the throat. "Thy false skin is honester than thyself, and warned us. Back inside!"

The robber's eyes shrivelled to the size of a snake's, as, with no tenderness, the youth grappled with him still entangled, and with hands, feet, and knees drove him into his shell as a hasty traveller tramples his effects into a packing-case.

"See," said Elaine, "how pleasantly we two have you at our disposal. Shall the neighbours be called to have a sight of the Dragon?"

"What do you want with me?" said Sir Francis, quietly. For he was a philosopher.

"In the first place," answered Geoffrey, "know that thou art caught. And if I shall spare thee this night, it may well be they'll set thy carcase swinging on the gallows-tree to-morrow morning,— or, being Christmas, the day after."

"I can see my case without thy help," Sir Francis replied. "What next?"

At this, Elaine came to Geoffrey and they whispered together.

"Thy trade is done for," said the youth, at length. "There'll be no more monks of Oyster-le-Main, and no more Dragon of Wantley. But thou and the other curs may live, if ye so choose."

"Through what do I buy my choice?"

"Through a further exhibition of thine art. Thou must play Dragon to-night once again for the last time. This, that I may show thee captive to Sir Godfrey Disseisin."

"And in chains, I think," added Elaine. "There is one

The Dragon perceiueth hymself to be entrapped

behind the post." It had belonged in the bear-pit during the
lives of Orlando Crumb and Furioso Bun, two bears trapped
expressly for the Baron near Roncevaux.

"After which?" inquired Sir Francis.

"Thou shalt go free, and I will claim this lady's hand from her
father, who promised her to any man that brought the Dragon to
him dead or alive."

"Papa shall be kept at a distance from you," said Elaine, "and
will never suspect in this dimness, if you roar at him thoroughly."

"Then," continued Geoffrey, "I shall lead thee away as my spoil,
and the people shall see the lizard-skin after a little while. But
thou must journey far from Wantley, and never show face again."

"And go from Oyster-le-Main and the tithings?" exclaimed Sir
Francis. "My house and my sustenance?"

"Sustain thyself elsewhere," said Geoffrey; "I care not how."

"No!" said Sir Francis. "I'll not do this."

"Then we call Sir Godfrey. The Baron will not love thee very
much, seeing how well he loves his Burgundy thou hast drank.
Thou gavest him sermons on cold spring-water. He'll remember
that. I think thou'lt be soon hanging. So choose."

The Knight of the Voracious Stomach was silent.

"This is a pretty scheme thou hast," he presently said. "And
not thine own. She has taught thee this wit, I'll be bound. Mated
to her thou'lt prosper, I fear."

"Come, thy choice," said Geoffrey, sternly.

A sour smile moved the lips of Sir Francis. "Well," he said,
"it has been good while it lasted. Yes, I consent. Our interests
lie together. See how Necessity is the mother of Friendship, also."

The mask was drawn over his face, and they wound the chain
about the great body.

"There must be sounds of fighting," said Elaine. "Make them
when I am gone into the house."

"If I had strangled thee in thy prison, which was in my mind," said the voice of the hidden speaker, "this folly we—but there. Let it go, and begin."

Then they fell to making a wonderful disturbance. The Dragon's voice was lifted in horrid howlings; and the young knight continually bawled with all his lungs. They chased as children in a game do: forward, back, and across to nowhere, knocking the barrels, clanking and clashing, up between the rows and around corners; and the dry earth was ground under their feet and swept from the floor upward in a fine floating yellow powder that they sucked down into their windpipes, while still they hustled and jangled and banged and coughed and grew dripping wet, so the dust and the water mingled and ran black streams along their bodies from the neck downwards, tickling their backs and stomachs mightily. When the breath was no longer inside them, they stopped to listen.

The house was stone still, and no noise came, save always the wind's same cheerless blowing.

"How much more of this before they will awaken?" exclaimed Geoffrey, in indignation. "'Tis a scandal people should sleep so."

"They are saying their prayers," said Sir Francis.

"It is a pity thou art such a miscreant," Geoffrey said, heartily; "otherwise I could sweat myself into a good-humour with thee."

But Sir Francis replied with coldness, "It is easy for the upper hand to laugh."

"We must at it again," said Geoffrey; "and this time I will let them hear thou art conquered." The din and hubbub recommenced. And Mistletoe could hear it where she quaked inside her closet holding the door with both hands. And the Baron could hear it He was locked in the bath-room, dreadfully sorry he had not gone to the Crusade. Quite unknowingly in his alarm he had laid hold of a cord that set going the shower-bath; but he gave no heed at all to this trifle. And every man and woman in the house heard the riot, from the scullion up through the cook to Popham, who had unstrapped his calves before retiring, so that now his lean shanks knocked together like hockey-sticks. Little Whelpdale, freezing in his shirt-tail under the bed, was crying piteously upon all Saints to forget about his sins and deliver him. Only Miss Elaine standing in her room listened with calm; and she with not much, being on the threshold of a chance that might turn untoward so readily. Presently a victorious shouting came from far down through the dark.

"He is mine!" the voice bellowed. "I have laid him low. The Dragon is taken." At this she hastened to summon Sir Godfrey.

"Why, where can he be?" she exclaimed, stopping in astonishment at his room, empty and the door open wide.

Down in the cellar the voice continued to call on all people to come and see the Dragon of Wantley. Also Elaine heard a splashing and dripping that sounded in the bath-room. So she ran to the door and knocked.

"You can't come in!" said the Baron angrily.

"Papa! They've caught the Dragon. Oh why are you taking your bath at such a time?"

"Taking my grandmother!" Sir Godfrey retorted in great dudgeon. But he let the rope go, and the shower stopped running. "Go to your room," he added. "I told you to lock your door. This Dragon——"

"But he's caught, papa," cried Elaine through the key-hole. "Don't you hear me? Geoff—— somebody has got him."

"How now?" said the Baron, unlocking the door and peering out. "What's all this?"

His dressing-gown was extremely damp, for stray spouts from the shower-bath had squirted over him. Fortunately, the breast-plate underneath had kept him dry as far as it went.

8

"Hum," he said, after he had listened to the voice in the cellar. "This is something to be cautious over."

"If the people of this house do not come soon to bear witness of my conquest," said the voice in tones of thunder, "I'll lead this Dragon through every chamber of it myself."

"Damnum absque injuria!" shrieked Sir Godfrey, and uttered much more horrible language entirely unfit for general use. "What the Jeofailes does the varlet mean by threatening an Englishman in his own house? I should like to know who lives here? I should like to know who I am?"

The Baron flew down the entry in a rage. He ran to his bedside and pulled his sword from under the pillows where he always kept it at night with his sun-dial.

"We shall see who is master of this house," he said. "I am not going to—does he suppose anybody that pleases can come carting their dragons through my premises? Get up! Get up! Every one!" he shouted, hurrying along the hall with the sword in his right hand and a lantern in his left. His slippers were only half on, so they made a slithering and slapping over the floor; and his speed was such that the quilted red dressing-gown filled with the wind and spread behind him till he looked like a huge new sort of bird or an eccentric balloon. Up and down in all quarters of the house went Sir Godfrey, pounding against every shut door. Out they came. Mistletoe from her closet, squeaking. Whelpdale from under his bed. The Baron allowed him time to put on a pair of breeches wrong side out. The cook came, and you could hear her panting all the way down from the attic. Out came the nine housemaids with hair in curl-papers. The seven footmen followed. Meeson and Welsby had forgotten their wigs. The coachman and grooms and stable-boys came in horse-blankets and boots. And last in the procession, old Popham, one calf securely strapped on, and the other dangling disgracefully. Breathless they

huddled behind the Baron, who strode to
the cellar, where he flung the door open.
Over in a corner was a hideous monster,
and every man fell against his neighbour
and shrieked. At which the monster
roared most alarmingly, and all fell together again. Young Geoffrey stood in
the middle of the cellar, and
said not a word. One end of
a chain was in his hand, and
he waited mighty stiff for the
Baron to speak. But when he
saw Miss

Elaine come stealing in after the
rest so quiet and with her eyes
fixed upon him, his own eyes shone
wonderfully.

At the sight of the Dragon, Sir
Godfrey forgot his late excitement,
and muttered "Bless my soul!"
Then he stared at the beast for
some time.

"Can—can't he do anything?"
he inquired.

"No," said Geoffrey shortly; "he can't."

"Not fly up at one, for instance?"

"I have broken his wing," replied the
youth.

"I—I'd like to look at him. Never saw
one before," said the Baron; and he took
two steps. Then gingerly he moved another step.

"Take care!" Geoffrey cried, with rapid alarm.

The monster moved, and from his nostrils (as it seemed) shot a plume of flame.

Popham clutched the cook, and the nine house-maids sank instantly into the arms of the seven footmen without the slightest regard to how unsatisfactorily nine goes into seven.

"Good heavens!" said the Baron, getting behind a hogshead, "what a brute!"

"Perhaps it might be useful if I excommunicated him," said the Rev. Hucbald, who had come in rather late, with his clerical frock-coat buttoned over his pyjamas.

"Pooh!" said the Baron. "As if he'd care for that."

"Very few men can handle a dragon," said Geoffrey, unconcernedly, and stroked his upper lip, where a kindly-disposed person might see there was going to be a moustache some day.

"I don't know exactly what you mean to imply by that, young man," said the Baron, coming out from behind the hogshead and puffing somewhat pompously.

"Why, zounds!" he exclaimed, "I left you locked up this afternoon, and securely. How came you here?"

Geoffrey coughed, for it was an awkward inquiry.

"Answer me without so much throat-clearing," said the Baron.

"I'll clear my throat as it pleases me," replied Geoffrey hotly. "How I came here is no affair of yours that I can see. But ask Father Anselm himself, and he will tell you." This was a happy thought, and the youth threw a look at the Dragon, who nodded slightly. "I have a question to ask you, sir," Geoffrey continued, taking a tone and manner more polite. Then he pointed to the Dragon with his sword, and was silent.

"Well?" said Sir Godfrey, "don't keep me waiting."

"I fear your memory's short, sir. By your word proclaimed this morning the man who brought you this Dragon should have your daughter to wife if she—if she——"

"Ha!" said the Baron. "To be sure. Though it was hasty. Hum! Had I foreseen the matter would be so immediately settled —she's a great prize for any lad—and you're not hurt either. One should be hurt for such a reward. You seem entirely sound of limb and without a scratch. A great prize."

"There's the Dragon," replied Geoffrey, "and here am I."

Now Sir Godfrey was an honourable man. When he once had given his word, you could hold him to it. That is very uncommon to-day, particularly in the matter of contracts. He gathered his dressing-gown about him, and looked every inch a parent. "Elaine," he said, "my dear?"

"Oh, papa!" murmured that young woman in a die-away voice.

Geoffrey had just time to see the look in her brown eye as she turned her head away. And his senses reeled blissfully, and his brain blew out like a candle, and he ceased to be a man who could utter speech. He stood stock-still with his gaze fixed upon Elaine. The nine house-maids looked at the young couple with many sympathetic though respectful sighings, and the seven foot-men looked comprehensively at the nine house-maids.

Sir Godfrey smiled, and very kindly. "Ah, well," he said, "once I—but tush! You're a brave lad, and I knew your father well. I'll consent, of course. But if you don't mind, I'll give you rather a quick blessing this evening. 'Tis growing colder. Come here, Elaine. Come here, sir. There! Now, I hate delay in these matters. You shall be married to-morrow. Hey? What? You don't object I suppose? Then why did you jump? To-morrow, Christmas Day, and every church-bell in the county shall ring three times more than usual. Once for the holy Feast, and may the Lord bless it always! and once for my girl's wedding. And once for the death and destruction of the Dragon of Wantley."

"Hurrah!" said the united household.

"We'll have a nuptials that shall be the talk of our grand-

children's children, and after them. We'll have all the people to
see. And we'll build the biggest pile of fagots that can be cut
from my timber, and the Dragon shall be chained on the top of
it, and we'll cremate him like an Ancient,—only alive! We'll
cremate the monster alive!"

Elaine jumped. Geoffrey jumped. The chain round the Dragon
loudly clanked.

"Why—do you not find this a pleasant plan?" asked the Baron,
surprised.

"It seems to me, sir," stuttered Geoffrey, beating his brains for
every next word, "it seems to me a monstrous pity to destroy this
Dragon so. He is a rare curiosity."

"Did you expect me to clap him in a box-stall and feed him?"
inquired the Baron with scorn.

"Why, no sir. But since it is I who have tracked, stalked, and
taken him with the help of no other huntsman," said Geoffrey, "I
make bold to think the laws of sport vest the title to him in me."

"No such thing," said Sir Godfrey. "You have captured him
in my cellar. I know a little law, I hope."

"The law about wild beasts in Poictiers——" Geoffrey began.

"What care I for your knavish and perverted foreign legalities
over the sea?" snorted Sir Godfrey. "This is England. And our
Common Law says you have trespassed."

"My dear sir," said Geoffrey, "this wild beast came into your
premises after I had marked him."

"Don't dear sir me!" shouted the Baron. "Will you hear the
law for what I say? I tell you this Dragon's my dragon. Don't
I remember how trespass was brought against Ralph de Coventry,
over in Warwickshire? Who did no more than you have done.
And they held him. And there it was but a little pheasant his
hawk had chased into another's warren—and you've chased a
dragon, so the offence is greater."

"But if—" remonstrated the youth, "if a fox——"

"Fox me no foxes! Here is the case of Ralph de Coventry," replied Sir Godfrey, looking learned, and seating himself on a barrel of beer. "Ralph pleaded before the Judge saying, 'et nous lessamus nostre faucon voler à luy, et il le pursuy en le garrein,' —'tis just your position, only 'twas you that pursued and not your falcon, which does not in the least distinguish the cases."

"But," said Geoffrey again, "the Dragon started not on your premises."

"No matter for that; for you have pursued him into my warren, that is, my cellar, my enclosed cellar, where you had no business to be. And the Court told Ralph no matter 'que le feisant leva hors de le garrein, vostre faucon luy pursuy en le garrein.' So there's good sound English law, and none of your foppish outlandishries in Latin," finished the Baron, vastly delighted at being able to display the little learning that he had. For you see, very few gentlemen in those benighted days knew how to speak the beautiful language of the law so fluently as that.

"And besides," continued Sir Godfrey suddenly, "there is a contract."

"What contract?" asked Geoffrey.

"A good and valid one. When I said this morning that I would give my daughter to the man who brought me the Dragon alive or dead, did I say I would give him the Dragon too? So choose which you will take, for both you cannot have."

At this Elaine turned pale as death, and Geoffrey stood dumb.

Had anybody looked at the Dragon, it was easy to see the beast was much agitated.

"Choose!" said Sir Godfrey. "'Tis getting too cold to stay here. What? You hesitate between my daughter and a miserable reptile? I thought the lads of France were more gallant. Come, sir! which shall it be? The lady or the Dragon?

"Well," said Geoffrey, and his blood and heart stood still (and so did Elaine's, and so did another person's), "I—I—think I will choose the I—lady."

"Hurrah!" cheered the household once more.

"Oh, Lord!" said the Dragon, but nobody heard him.

"Indeed!" observed Sir Godfrey. "And now we'll chain him in my bear-pit till morning, and at noon he shall be burned alive by the blazing fagots. Let us get some sleep now."

The cloud of slimly-clad domestics departed with slow steps, and many a look of fear cast backward at the captured monster.

"This Dragon, sir," said Geoffrey, wondering at his own voice, "will die of thirst in that pit. Bethink you how deep is his habit of drinking."

"Ha! I have often bethought me," retorted Sir Godfrey, rolling his eyes over the empty barrels. "But here! I am a man of some heart, I hope."

He seized up a bucket and ran to the hogshead containing his daughter's native cowslip wine.

"There!" he observed when the bucket was pretty well filled. "Put that in to moisten his last hours."

Then the Baron led the way round the Manor to the courtyard where the bear-pit was. His daughter kept pace with him not easily, for the excellent gentleman desired to be a decent distance away from the Dragon, whom young Geoffrey dragged along in the rear.

·HVCBALD· BELIEVES·
HE·WILL· ·TAKE·
·JVST· ·A·

·LITTLE·
·SIP·

CHAPTER IX

AS they proceeded towards the bear-pit, having some distance to go, good-humour and benevolence began to rise up in the heart of Sir Godfrey.

"This is a great thing!" he said to Miss Elaine. "Ha! an important and joyful occurrence. The news of it will fly far."

"Yes," the young lady replied, but without enthusiasm. "The cattle will be safe now."

"The cattle, child! my Burgundy! Think of that!"

"Yes, papa."

"The people will come," continued the Baron, "from all sides to-morrow—why, it's to-morrow now!" he cried. "From all sides they will come to my house to see my Dragon. And I shall permit them to see him. They shall see him cooked alive, if they wish. It is a very proper curiosity. The brute had a wide reputation."

To hear himself spoken of in the past tense, as we speak of the dead, was not pleasant to Sir Francis, walking behind Geoffrey on all fours.

"I shall send for Father Anselm and his monks," the Baron went on.

Hearing this Geoffrey started.

"What need have we of them, sir?" he inquired. To send for Father Anselm! It was getting worse and worse.

"Need of Father Anselm?" repeated Sir Godfrey. "Of course
I shall need him. I want the parson to tell me how he came to
change his mind and let you out."

"Oh, to be sure," said Geoffrey mechanically. His thoughts
were reeling helplessly together, with no one thing uppermost.

"Not that I disapprove it. I have changed my own mind upon
occasions. But 'twas sudden, after his bundle of sagacity about
Crusades and visions of my ancestor and what not over there in
the morning. Ha! ha! These clericals are no more consistent
than another person. I'll never let the Father forget this." And
the Baron chuckled. "Besides," he said, "'tis suitable that these
monks should be present at the burning. This Dragon was a
curse, and curses are somewhat of a church matter."

"True," said Geoffrey, for lack of a better reply.

"Why, bless my soul!" shouted the Baron, suddenly wheeling
round to Elaine at his side, so that the cowslip wine splashed out
of the bucket he carried, "it's my girl's wedding-day too! I had
clean forgot. Bless my soul!"

"Y—yes, papa," faltered Elaine.

"And you, young fellow!" her father called out to Geoffrey
with lusty heartiness. "You're a lucky rogue, sir."

"Yes, sir," said Geoffrey, but not gayly. He was wondering
how it felt to be going mad. Amid his whirling thoughts burned
the one longing to hide Elaine safe in his arms and tell her it
would all come right somehow. A silence fell on the group as
they walked. Even to the Baron, who was not a close observer,
the present reticence of these two newly-betrothed lovers was
apparent. He looked from one to the other, but in the face of
neither could he see beaming any of the soft transports which he
considered were traditionally appropriate to the hour. "Umph!" he
exclaimed; "it was never like this in my day." Then his thoughts
went back some forty years, and his eyes mellowed from within.

"We'll cook the Dragon first," continued the old gentleman, "and then, sir, you and my girl shall be married. Ha! ha! a great day for Wantley!" The Baron swung his bucket, and another jet of its contents slid out. He was growing more and more delighted with himself and his daughter and her lover and everybody in the world. "And you're a stout rogue, too, sir," he said. "Built near as well as an Englishman, I think. And that's an excellent thing in a husband."

The Baron continued to talk, now and then almost falling in the snow, but not permitting such slight mishaps to interrupt his discourse, which was addressed to nobody and had a general nature, touching upon dragons, marriages, Crusades, and Burgundy. Could he have seen Geoffrey's more and more woe-begone and distracted expression, he would have concluded his future son-in-law was suffering from some sudden and momentous bodily ill.

The young man drew near the Dragon. "What shall we do?" he said in a whisper. "Can I steal the keys of the pit? Can we say the Dragon escaped?" The words came in nervous haste, wholly unlike the bold deliberateness with which the youth usually spoke. It was plain he was at the end of his wits.

"Why, what ails thee?" inquired Sir Francis in a calm and unmoved voice. "This is a simple matter."

His tone was so quiet that Geoffrey stared in amazement.

"But yonder pit!" he said. "We are ruined!"

"Not at all," Sir Francis replied. "Truly thou art a deep thinker! First a woman and now thine enemy has to assist thy distress."

He put so much hatred and scorn into his tones that Geoffrey flamed up. "Take care!" he muttered angrily.

"That's right!" the prisoner said, laughing dryly. "Draw thy sword and split our secret open. It will be a fine wedding-day thou'lt have then. Our way out of this is plain enough. Did not the Baron say that Father Anselm was to be present at the burning? He shall be present."

"Yes," said the youth. "But how to get out of the pit? And how can there be a dragon to burn if thou art to be Father Anselm? And how——" he stopped.

"I am full of pity for thy brains," said Sir Francis.

"Here's the pit!" said the voice of Sir Godfrey. "Bring him along."

"Hark!" said Sir Francis to Geoffrey. "Thou must go to Oyster-le-Main with a message. Darest thou go alone?"

"If I dare?" retorted Geoffrey, proudly.

"It is well. Come to the pit when the Baron is safe in the house."

Now they were at the iron door. Here the ground was on a level with the bottom of the pit, but sloped steeply up to the top of its walls elsewhere, so that one could look down inside. The Baron unlocked the door and entered with his cowslip wine, which (not being a very potent decoction) began to be covered with threads of ice as soon as it was set down. The night was growing more bitter as its frosty hours wore on; for the storm was departed, and the wind fallen to silence, and the immense sky clean and cold with the shivering glitter of the stars.

Then Geoffrey led the Dragon into the pit. This was a rude and desolate hole, and its furniture of that extreme simplicity common to bear-pits in those barbarous times. From the middle of the stone floor rose the trunk of a tree, ragged with lopped boughs and at its top forking into sundry limbs possible to sit among. An iron trough was there near a heap of stale greasy straw, and both were shapeless white lumps beneath the snow. The chiselled and cemented walls rose round in a circle and showed no crevice for the nails of either man or bear to climb by. Many times had Orlando Crumb and Furioso Bun observed this with sadness, and now Sir Francis observed it also. He took into his chest a big swallow of air, and drove it out again between his teeth with a weary hissing.

"I will return at once." Geoffrey whispered as he was leaving.

Then the door was shut to, and Sir Francis heard the lock grinding as the key was turned. Then he heard the Baron speaking to Geoffrey.

"I shall take this key away," he said; "there's no telling what wandering fool might let the monster out. And now there's but little time before dawn. Elaine, child, go to your bed. This excitement has plainly tired you. I cannot have my girl look like that when she's a bride to-day. And you too, sir," he added, surveying Geoffrey, "look a trifle out of sorts. Well, I am not surprised. A dragon is no joke. Come to my study." And he took Geoffrey's arm.

"Oh, no!" said the youth. "I cannot. I—I must change my dress."

"Pooh, sir! I shall send to the tavern for your kit. Come to my study. You are pale. We'll have a little something hot. Aha! Something hot!"

"But I think——" Geoffrey began.

"Tush!" said the Baron. "You shall help me with the wedding invitations."

"Sir!" said Geoffrey haughtily, "I know nothing of writing and such low habits."

"Why no more do I, of course." replied Sir Godfrey: "nor would I suspect you or any good gentleman of the practice, though I have made my mark upon an indenture in the presence of witnesses."

"A man may do that with propriety." assented the youth, "But I cannot come with you now, sir. 'Tis not possible."

"But I say that you shall!" cried the Baron in high good-

Sir Francis
decideth to go
down agayne

humour. "I can mull Malvoisie famously, and will presently do so for you. 'Tis to help me seal the invitations that I want you. My Chaplain shall write them. Come."

He locked Geoffrey's arm in his own, and strode quickly forward Feeling himself dragged away, Geoffrey turned his head despairingly back towards the pit.

"Oh, he's safe enough in there," said Sir Godfrey. "No need to watch him."

Sir Francis had listened to this conversation with rising dismay. And now he quickly threw off the crocodile hide and climbed up the tree as the bears had often done before him. It came almost to a level with the wall's rim, but the radius was too great a distance for jumping.

"I should break my leg," he said, and came down the tree again, as the bears had likewise often descended.

The others were now inside the house. Elaine with a sinking heart retired to her room, and her father after summoning the Rev. Hucbald took Geoffrey into his study. The Chaplain followed with a bunch of goose-quills and a large ink-horn, and seated himself at a table, while the Baron mixed some savoury stuff, going down his private staircase into the buttery to get the spice and honey necessary.

"Here's to the health of all, and luck to-day," said the Baron; and Geoffrey would have been quite happy if an earthquake had come and altered all plans for the morning. Still he went through the form of clinking goblets. But his heart ached, and his eyes grew hot as he sat dismal and lonely away from his girl.

"Whom shall we ask to the wedding?" queried the Rev. Hucbald, rubbing his hands and looking at the pitcher in which Sir Godfrey had mixed the beverage.

"Ask the whole county," said Sir Godfrey. "The more the merrier. My boy Roland will be here to-morrow. He'll find his sister has got ahead of him. Have some?" he added, holding the pitcher to the Rev. Hucbald.

"I do believe I will take just a little sip," returned the divine. "Thanks! ah—most delicious, Baron! A marriage on Christmas Day," he added, "is—ahem!—highly irregular. But under the unusual, indeed the truly remarkable, circumstances, I make no doubt that the Pope——"

"Drat him!" said Sir Godfrey; at which the Chaplain smiled reproachfully, and shook a long transparent taper finger at his patron in a very playful manner, saying, "Baron! now Baron!"

"My boy Roland's learning to be a knight over at my uncle Mortmain's," continued Sir Godfrey, pouring Geoffrey another goblet. "You'll like him."

But Geoffrey's thoughts were breeding more anxiety in him every moment.

"I'll get the sealing-wax," observed the Baron, and went to a cabinet.

"This room is stifling," cried Geoffrey. "I shall burst soon, I think."

"It's my mulled Malvoisie you're not accustomed to," Sir Godfrey said, as he rummaged in the cabinet. "Open the window

9

and get some fresh air, my lad. Now where the deuce is my family seal?"

As Geoffrey opened the window, a soft piece of snow flew through the air and dropped lightly on his foot. He looked quickly and perceived a man's shadow jutting into the moonlight from an angle in the wall. Immediately he plunged out through the casement, which was not very high.

"Merciful powers!" said the Rev. Hucbald, letting fall his quill and spoiling the first invitation, "what an impulsive young man! Why he has run clean round the corner."

"'Tis all my Malvoisie," said the Baron, hugely delighted, and hurrying to the window. "Come back when you're sober!" he shouted after Geoffrey with much mirth. Then he shut the window.

"These French heads never can weather English brews," he remarked to the Chaplain. "But I'll train the boy in time. He is a rare good lad. Now, to work."

Out in the snow, Geoffrey with his sword drawn came upon Hubert.

"Thou mayest sheathe that knife," said the latter.

"And be thy quarry?" retorted Geoffrey.

"I have come too late for that!" Hubert answered.

"Thou hast been to the bear-pit, then?"

"Oh, aye!"

"There's big quarry there!" observed Geoffrey, tauntingly. "Quite a royal bird."

"So royal the male hawk could not bring it down by himself, I hear," Hubert replied. "Nay, there's no use in waxing wroth, friend! My death now would clap thee in a tighter puzzle than thou art in already—and I should be able to laugh down at thee from a better world," he added, mimicking the priestly cadence, and looking at Geoffrey half fierce and half laughing.

He was but an apprentice at robbery and violence, and in the bottom of his heart, where some honesty still was, he liked Geoffrey well. "Time presses," he continued. "I must go. One thing thou must do. Let not that pit be opened till the monks of Oyster-le-Main come here. We shall come before noon."

"I do not understand," said Geoffrey.

"That's unimportant," answered Hubert. "Only play thy part. 'Tis a simple thing to keep a door shut. Fail, and the whole of us are undone. Farewell."

"Nay, this is some foul trick," Geoffrey declared, and laid his hand on Hubert.

But the other shook his head sadly. "Dost suppose," he said, "that we should have abstained from any trick that's known to the accumulated wisdom of man? Our sport is up."

"'Tis true," Geoffrey said, musingly, "we hold all of you in the hollow of one hand."

"Thou canst make a present of us to the hangman in twenty minutes if thou choosest," said Hubert.

"Though 'twould put me in quite as evil case."

Brother Hvbert goeth back to Oyster-le-Main for y'last Time

"Ho! what's the loss of a woman compared with death?" Hubert exclaimed.

"Thou'lt know some day," the young knight said, eying Hubert with a certain pity; "that is, if ever thou art lucky to love truly."

"And is it so much as that?" murmured Hubert wistfully. "'Twas good fortune for thee and thy sweetheart I did not return to look for my master while he was being taken to the pit," he continued; "we could have stopped all your mouths till the Day of Judgment at least."

"Wouldst thou have slain a girl?" asked Geoffrey, stepping back.

"Not I, indeed! But for my master I would not be so sure. And he says I'll come as far as that in time," added the apprentice with a shade of bitterness.

"Thou art a singular villain," said Geoffrey, "and wonderfully frank spoken."

"And so thou'rt to be married," Hubert said gently.

"By this next noon, if all goes well!" exclaimed the lover with ardour.

"Heigho!" sighed Hubert, turning to go, "'twill be a merry Christmas for somebody."

"Give me thy hand," cried Geoffrey, feeling universally hearty.

"No," replied the freebooter; "what meaning would there be in that? I would sever thy jugular vein in a moment if that would mend the broken fortunes of my chief. Farewell, however. Good luck attend thee."

The eyes of both young men met, and without unkindness in them.

"But I am satisfied with my calling," Hubert asserted, repudiating some thought that he imagined was lurking in Geoffrey's look. "Quite content! It's very dull to be respectable. Look! the dawn will discover us."

"But this plan?" cried Geoffrey, hastening after him; "I know nothing."

"Thou needest know nothing. Keep the door of the pit shut. Farewell."

And Geoffrey found himself watching the black form of Hubert dwindle against the white rises of the ground. He walked towards the tavern in miserable uncertainty, for the brief gust of elation had passed from his heart. Then he returned irresolute, and looked into the pit. There was Sir Francis, dressed in the crocodile.

"Come in, come in, young fellow! Ha! ha! how's thy head?" The Baron was at the window, calling out and beckoning with vigour.

Geoffrey returned to the study. There was no help for it.

"We have written fifty-nine already!" said the Rev. Hucbald.

But the youth cast a dull eye upon the growing heap, and sealed them very badly. What pleasure was it to send out invitations to his own wedding that might never be coming off?

As for Hubert out in the night, he walked slowly through the wide white country. And as he went across the cold fields and saw how the stars were paling out, and cast long looks at the moon setting across the smooth snow, the lad's eyes filled so that the moon twinkled and shot rays askew in his sight. He thought how the good times of Oyster-le-Main were ended, and he thought of Miss Elaine so far beyond the reach of such as he, and it seemed to him that he was outside the comfortable world.

CHAPTER X

OW are all the people long awake and out of their beds. Wantley Manor is stirring busily in each quarter of the house and court, and the whole county likewise is agog. By seven o'clock this morning it was noised in every thatched cottage and in every gabled hall that the great Dragon had been captured. Some said by Saint George in person, who appeared riding upon a miraculous white horse and speaking a tongue that nobody could understand, wherefore it was held to be the language common in Paradise. Some declared Saint George had nothing to do with it, and that this was the pious achievement of Father Anselm. Others were sure Miss Elaine had fulfilled the legend and conquered the monster entirely by herself. One or two, hearing the event had taken place in Sir Godfrey's wine-cellar, said they thought the Baron had done it,— and were immediately set down as persons of unsound mind. But nobody mentioned Geoffrey at all, until the Baron's invitations, requesting the honour of various people's presence at the marriage of his daughter Elaine to that young man, were received; and that was about ten o'clock, the ceremony being named for twelve that day in the family chapel. Sir Godfrey intended the burning of the Dragon to take place not one minute later than half-past eleven. Accordingly, besides the invitation to the chapel, all friends and neighbours whose position in the county or whose intimacy with

the family entitled them to a recognition less formal and more
personal, received a second card which ran as follows: "Sir Godfrey Disseisin at home Wednesday morning, December the twenty-
fifth, from half after eleven until the following day. Dancing; also
a Dragon will be roasted. R. S. V. P." The Disseisin crest with
its spirited motto, "Saute qui peult," originated by the venerable
Primer Disseisin, followed by his son Tortious Disseisin, and borne
with so much renown in and out of a hundred battles by a thousand subsequent Disseisins, ornamented the top left-hand corner.

"I think we shall have but few refusals," said the Rev. Hucbald
to Sir Godfrey. "Not many will be prevented by previous engage-
ments, I opine." And the Chaplain smiled benignly, rubbing his
hands. He had published the banns of matrimony three times in
a lump before breakfast. "Which is rather unusual," he said: "but
under the circumstances we shall easily obtain a dispensation."

"In providing such an entertainment for the county as this will
be," remarked the Baron, "I feel I have performed my duty towards
society for some time to come. No one has had a dragon at a
private house before me, I believe."

"Oh surely not," simpered the sleek Hucbald. "Not even
Lady Jumping Jack."

"Fiddle!" grunted the Baron. "She indeed! Fandangoes!"

"She's very pious," protested the Rev. Hucbald, whom the lady
sometimes asked to fish lunches in Lent.

"Fandangoes!" repeated the Baron. He had once known her
exceedingly well, but she pursued variety at all expense, even his.
As for refusals, the Chaplain was quite right. There were none.
Nobody had a previous engagement—or kept it, if they had.

"Good gracious, Rupert!" (or Cecil, or Chandos, as it might be,)
each dame in the county had exclaimed to her lord on opening
the envelope brought by private hand from Wantley, "we're asked
to the Disseisins to see a dragon,—and his daughter married."

"By heaven, Muriel, we'll go!" the gentleman invariably replied,
under the impression that Elaine was to marry the Dragon, which
would be a show worth seeing. The answers came flying back to
Wantley every minute or two, most of them written in such haste
that you could only guess they were acceptances. And those indi-
viduals who lived so far away across the county that the invitations
reached them too late to be answered, immediately rang every bell
in the house and ordered the carriage in frantic tones.

Of *course* nobody kept any engagement. Sir Guy Vol-au-Vent
(and none but a most abandoned desperado or advanced thinker
would be willing to do such a thing on Christmas) had accepted
an invitation to an ambush at three for the slaying of Sir Percy
de Résistance. But the ambush was put off till a more convenient
day. Sir Thomas de Brie had been going to spend his Christmas at
a cock-fight in the Count de Gorgonzola's barn. But he remarked
to his man Edward, who brought the trap to the door, that the
Count de Gorgonzola might go—— Never mind what he remarked.
It was not nice; though oddly enough it was exactly the same
remark that the Count had made about Sir Thomas on telling his
own man James to drive to Wantley and drop the cock-fight. All
these gentlemen, as soon as they heard the great news, started for
the Manor with the utmost speed.

Nor was it the quality alone who were so unanimous in their
feelings. The Tenantry (to whom Sir Godfrey had extended a
very hospitable bidding to come and they should find standing-
room and good meat and beer in the court-yard) went nearly
mad. From every quarter of the horizon they came plunging and
ploughing along. The sun blazed down out of a sky whence a
universal radiance seemed to beat upon the blinding white. Could
you have mounted up bird-fashion over the country, you would
have seen the Manor like the centre of some great wheel, with
narrow tracks pointing in to it from the invisible rim of a circle,

paths wide and narrow, converging at the gate, trodden across the new snow from anywhere and everywhere; and moving along these like ants, all the inhabitants for miles around. And through the wide splendour of winter no wind blowing, but the sound of chiming bells far and near, clear frozen drops of music in the brittle air.

Old Gaffer Piers, the ploughman, stumped along, "pretty well for eighty, thanky," as he somewhat snappishly answered to the neighbours who out-walked him on the road. They would get there first.

"Wonderful old man," they said as they went on their way, and quickly resumed their speculations upon the Dragon's capture. Farmer John Stiles came driving his ox-team and snuffling, for it was pretty cold, and his handkerchief at home. Upon his wagon on every part, like swallows, hung as many of his relations as could get on. His mother, who had been Lucy Baker, and grandmother Cecilia Kempe, and a litter of cousin Thorpes. But his step-father Lewis Gay and the children of the half-blood were not asked to ride : farmer Stiles had bitterly resented the second marriage. This family knew all the particulars concerning the Dragon, for they had them from the cook's second cousin who was courting Bridget Stiles. They knew how Saint George had waked Father Anselm up and put him on a white horse, and how the Abbot had thus been able to catch the Dragon by his tail in the air just as he was flying away with Miss Elaine, and how at that the white horse had turned into a young man who had been bewitched by the Dragon, and was going to marry Miss Elaine immediately.

On the front steps, shaking hands with each person who came, was Sir Godfrey. He had dressed himself excellently for the occasion ; something between a heavy father and an old beau, with a beautiful part down the back of his head where the hair was. Geoffrey stood beside him.

"My son-in-law that's to be," Sir Godfrey would say. And the gentry welcomed the young man, while the tenants bobbed him respectful salutations.

"You're one of us. Glad to know you," said Sir Thomas de Brie, surveying the lad with approval.

Lady Jumping Jack held his hand for a vanishing moment you could hardly make sure of. "I had made up my mind to hate you for robbing me of my dearest girl," she said, smiling gayly, and fixing him with her odd-looking eyes. "But I see we're to be friends." Then she murmured a choice nothing to the Baron, who snarled politely.

"Don't let her play you," said he to Geoffrey when the lady had moved on. And he tapped the youth's shoulder familiarly.

"Oh I've been through all that sort of thing over in Poictiers," Geoffrey answered with indifference.

"You're a rogue, sir, as I've told you before. Ha! Uncle Mortmain, how d'ye do? Yes, this is Geoffrey. Where's my boy

Roland? Coming, is he? Well, he had better look sharp. It's after eleven, and I'll wait for nobody. How d'ye do, John Stiles? That bull you sold me 's costing thirty shillings a year in fences. You'll find something ready down by those tables, I think."

Hark to that roar! The crowd jostled together in the court-yard, for it sounded terribly close.

"The Dragon's quite safe in the pit, good people," shouted Sir Godfrey. "A few more minutes and you'll all see him."

The old gentleman continued welcoming the new arrivals, chatting heartily, with a joke for this one and a kind inquiry for the other. But wretched Geoffrey! So the Dragon was to be seen in a few minutes! And where were the monks of Oyster-le-Main? Still, a bold face must be kept. He was thankful that Elaine, after the custom of brides, was invisible. The youth's left hand rested upon the hilt of his sword; he was in rich attire, and the curly hair that surrounded his forehead had been carefully groomed. Half-way up the stone steps as he stood, his blue eyes watching keenly for the monks, he was a figure that made many a humble nymph turn tender glances upon him. Old Piers, the ploughman, remained beside a barrel of running ale and drank his health all day. For he was a wonderful old man.

Hither and thither the domestics scurried swiftly, making preparations. Some were cooking rare pasties of grouse and ptarmigan, goslings and dough-birds; some were setting great tables in-doors and out; and some were piling fagots for the Dragon's funeral pyre. Popham, with magnificent solemnity and a pair of new calves, gave orders to Meeson and Welsby, and kept little Whelpdale panting for breath with errands; while in and out, between everybody's legs, and over or under all obstacles, stalked the two ravens Croak James and Croak Elizabeth, a big white wedding-favour tied round the neck of each. To see these grave birds, none would have suspected how frequently they had been in the

mince-pies that morning, though Popham had expressly ruled (in
somewhat stilted language) that they should "take nothink by their
bills."

"Geoffrey," said the Baron, "I think we'll begin. Popham, tell
them to light that fire there."

"The guests are still coming, sir," said Geoffrey.

"No matter. It is half after eleven." The Baron showed his
sun-dial, and there was no doubt of it. "Here, take the keys," he
said, "and bring the monster out for us."

"I'll go and put on my armour," suggested the young man.
That would take time; perhaps the monks might arrive.

"Why the brute's chained. You need no armour. Nonsense!"

"But think of my clothes in that pit, sir,—on my wedding-day."

"Pooh! That's the first sign of a Frenchman I've seen in you.
Take the keys, sir."

The crackle of the kindling fagots came to Geoffrey's ears. He
saw the forty men with chains that were to haul the Dragon into
the fire.

"But there's Father Anselm yet to come," he protested.
"Surely we wait for him."

"I'll wait for nobody. He with his Crusades and rubbish!
Haven't I got this Dragon, and there's no Crusade?—Ah, Cousin
Modus, glad you could come over. Just in time. The sherry's to

your left. Yes, it's a very fine day. Yes, yes, this is Geoffrey my girl's to marry and all that.—What do I care about Father Anselm?" the old gentleman resumed testily, when his cousin Modus had shuffled off. "Come, sir."

He gave the keys into Geoffrey's unwilling hand, and ordered silence proclaimed.

"Hearken, good friends!" said he, and all talk and going to and fro ceased. The tenantry stood down in the court-yard, a mass of motionless russet and yellow, every face watching the Baron. The gentry swarmed noiselessly out upon the steps behind him, their handsome dresses bright against the Manor walls. There was a short pause. Old Gaffer Piers made a slight disturbance falling over with his cup of ale, but was quickly set on his feet by his neighbours. The sun blazed down, and the growling of the Dragon came from the pit.

"Yonder noise," pursued Sir Godfrey, "speaks more to the point than I could. I'll give you no speech." All loudly cheered at this.

"Don't you think," whispered the Rev. Hucbald in the Baron's ear, "that a little something serious should be said on such an occasion? I should like our brethren to be reminded——"

"Fudge!" said the Baron. "For thirteen years," he continued, raising his voice again, "this Dragon has been speaking for himself. You all know and I know how that has been. And now we are going to speak for ourselves. And when he is on top of that fire he'll know how that is. Geoffrey, open the pit and get him out."

Again there was a cheer, but a short one, for the spell of expectancy was on all. The young man descended into the court, and the air seemed to turn to a wavering mist as he looked up at the Manor windows seeking to spy Elaine's face at one of them. Was this to be the end? Could he kiss her one last good-by if

disaster was in store for them after all? Alas! no glimpse of her
was to be seen as he moved along, hardly aware of his own steps,
and the keys jingling lightly as he moved. Through the crowd he
passed, and a whispering ran in his wake followed by deeper
silence than before. He reached the edge of the people and
crossed the open space beyond, passing the leaping blaze of the
fagots, and so drew near the iron door of the pit. The key went
slowly into the lock. All shrank with dismay at the roar which
rent the air. Geoffrey paused with his hand gripping the key, and
there came a sound of solemn singing over the fields.

"The monks!" murmured a few under their breath; and silence
fell again, each listening.

Men's voices it was, and their chanting rose by one sudden
step to a high note that was held for a moment, and then sank
again, mellow like the harmony of horns in a wood. Then over
the ridge from Oyster-le-Main the length of a slow procession
began to grow. The gray gowns hung to the earth straight with
scarce any waving as the men walked. The heavy hoods reached
over each face so there was no telling its features. None in the
court-yard spoke at all, as the brooding figures passed in under the
gateway and proceeded to the door of the bear-pit, singing always.
Howlings that seemed born of terror now rose from the imprisoned
monster; and many thought, "evidently the evil beast cannot
endure the sound of holy words."

Elaine in her white dress now gazed from an upper window,
seeing her lover with his enemies drawing continually closer around
him.

Perhaps it was well for him that his death alone would not
have served to lock their secret up again; that the white maiden
in the window is ready to speak the word and direct instant ven-
geance on them and their dragon if any ill befall that young man
who stands by the iron door.

The song of the monks ended. Sir Godfrey on the steps was
wondering why Father Anselm did not stand out from the rest of
the gray people and explain his wishes. "Though he shall not
interrupt the sport, whatever he says," thought the Baron, and
cast on the group of holy men a less hospitable eye than had
beamed on his other guests. Geoffrey over at the iron door,
surrounded by the motionless figures, scanned each hood narrowly
and soon met the familiar eyes of Hubert. Hubert's gown, he
noticed, bulged out in a manner ungainly and mysterious. "Open
the door," whispered that youth. At once Geoffrey began to turn
the key. And at its grinding all held their breath, and a quivering
silence hung over the court. The hasty drops pattered down from
the eaves from the snow that was melting on the roof. Then some
strip of metal inside the lock sprung suddenly, making a sharp
song, and ceased. The crowd of monks pressed closer together
as the iron door swung open.

What did Geoffrey see? None but the monks could tell. Instantly a single roar more terrible than any burst out, and the
huge horrible black head and jaws of the monster reared into the
view of Sir Godfrey and his guests. One instant the fearful vision
in the door-way swayed with a stiff strange movement over the
knot of monks that surrounded it, then sank out of sight among
them. There was a sound of jerking and fierce clanking of chains,
mingled with loud chanting of pious sentences. Then a plume of
spitting flame flared upward with a mighty roar, and the gray
figures scattered right and left. There along the ground lay the
monster, shrivelled, twisted in dismal coils, and dead. Close beside
his black body towered Father Anselm, smoothing the folds of
his gray gown. Geoffrey was sheathing his sword and looking at
Hubert, whose dress bulged out no longer, but fitted him as usual.

"We have been vouchsafed a miracle," said Father Anselm
quietly, to the gaping spectators.

"There'll be no burning," said
Geoffrey, pointing to the shrunken
skin. But though he spoke so coolly,
and repelled all besieging disturbance
from the fortress of his calm visage
and bearing, as a bold and haughty
youth should do, yet he could scarcely
hold his finger steady as it pointed to
the blackened carcase. Then all at
once his eyes met those of Elaine
where she watched from her window,
and relief and joy rushed through him.
He stretched his arms towards her,
not caring who saw, and the look she
sent him with a smile drove all sur-
rounding things to an immeasurable
distance away.

"Here indeed," Father Anselm
repeated, "is a miracle. Lo, the
empty shell! The snake hath shed
his skin."

THE • DRAGON • MAKETH • HIS • LAST • APPEARANCE

"This is very disappointing," said Sir Godfrey, bewildered. "Is there no dragon to roast?"

"The roasting," replied the Abbot impressively, "is even now begun for all eternity." He stretched out an arm and pointed downward through the earth. "The evil spirit has fled. The Church hath taken this matter into her own hands, and claims yon barren hide as a relic."

"Well,—I don't see why the Church can't let good sport alone," retorted Sir Godfrey.

"Hope she'll not take to breaking up my cock-fights this way," muttered the Count de Gorgonzola, sulkily.

"The Church cares nothing for such profane frivolities," observed Father Anselm with cold dignity.   .

"At all events, friends," said Sir Godfrey, cheering up, "the country is rid of the Dragon of Wantley, and we've got a wedding and a breakfast left."

Just at this moment a young horseman rode furiously into the court-yard.

It was Roland, Sir Godfrey's son. "Great news!" he began at once. "Another Crusade has been declared—and I am going. Merry Christmas! Where's Elaine? Where's the Dragon?"

Father Anselm's quick brain seized this chance. He and his monks should make a more stately exit than he had planned.

"See," he said in a clear voice to his monks, "how all is coming true that was revealed to me this night! My son," he continued, turning to young Roland, "thy brave resolve reached me ere thou hadst made it. Know it has been through thee that the Dragon has gone!"

Upon this there was profound silence.

"And now," he added solemnly, "farewell. The monks of Oyster-le-Main go hence to the Holy Land also, to battle for the true Faith. Behold! we have made us ready to meet the toil."

His haughty tones ceased, and he made a sign. The gray gowns fell to the snow, and revealed a stalwart, fierce-looking crew in black armour. But the Abbot kept his gray gown.

"You'll stay for the wedding?" inquired Sir Godfrey of him.

"Our duty lies to the sea. Farewell, for I shall never see thy face again."

He turned. Hubert gathered up the hide of the crocodile and threw a friendly glance back at Geoffrey. Then again raising their song, the black band slowly marched out under the gate and away over the snow until the ridge hid them from sight, and only their singing could be heard in the distant fields.

"Well," exclaimed Sir Godfrey, "it's no use to stand staring. Now for the wedding! Mistletoe, go up and tell Miss Elaine. Huebald, tell the organist to pipe up his music. And as soon as it's over we'll drink the bride's health and health to the bridegroom. 'Tis a lucky thing that between us all the Dragon is gone, for there's still enough of my Burgundy to last us till midnight. Come, friends, come in, for everything waits your pleasure!"

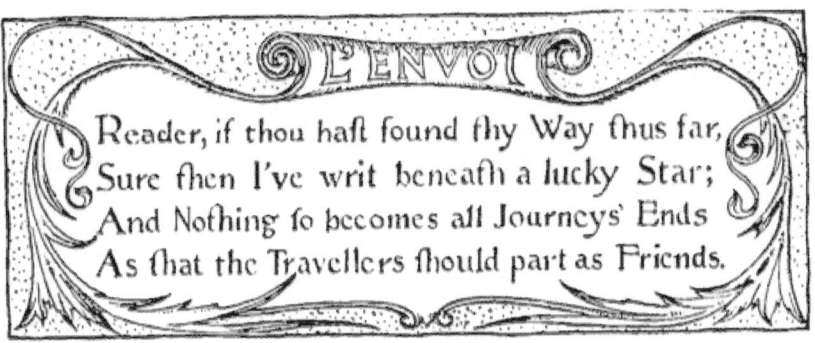

L'ENVOI

Reader, if thou haſt found thy Way thus far,
Sure then I've writ beneath a lucky Star;
And Nothing ſo becomes all Journeys' Ends
As that the Travellers ſhould part as Friends.

www.ingramcontent.com/pod-product-compliance
Lightning Source LLC
Chambersburg PA
CBHW020235030726
47497CB00009B/3098